Alternate Plains

ALTERNATE PLAINS

STORIES OF PRAIRIE SPECULATIVE FICTION

Edited by
Darren Ridgley and Adam Petrash

Enfield & Wizenty
(an imprint of Great Plains Publications)
320 Rosedale Avenue
Winnipeg, MB R3L 1L8
www.greatplains.mb.ca

Great Plains Publications gratefully acknowledges the financial support provided for its publishing program by the Government of Canada through the Canada Book Fund; the Canada Council for the Arts; the Province of Manitoba through the Book Publishing Tax Credit and the Book Publisher Marketing Assistance Program; and the Manitoba Arts Council.

Design & Typography by Relish New Brand Experience
Printed in Canada by Friesens

Library and Archives Canada Cataloguing in Publication

Title: Alternate plains : stories of prairie speculative fiction / edited by Darren Ridgley and Adam Petrash.
Names: Ridgley, Darren, 1984- editor. | Petrash, Adam, 1984- editor.
Identifiers: Canadiana (print) 20210259981 | Canadiana (ebook) 20210260009 | ISBN 9781773370644 (softcover) | ISBN 9781773370651 (ebook)
Subjects: CSH: Science fiction Canadian (English)—Prairie Provinces. | CSH: Short stories, Canadian (English)—Prairie Provinces. | CSH: Canadian fiction (English)—Prairie Provinces. | CSH: Canadian fiction (English)—21st century. | LCGFT: Science fiction. | LCGFT: Short stories.
Classification: LCC PS8329.5.P7 A48 2021 | DDC C813/.087609971209052—dc23

TREES	WATER	ENERGY	SOLID WASTE	GREENHOUSE GASES
3 FULLY GROWN	260 GALLONS	1 MILLION BTUs	11 POUNDS	1,430 POUNDS

Environmental impact estimates were made using the Environmental Paper Network Paper Calculator 4.0. For more information visit www.papercalculator.org

Canada

Table of Contents

Foreword

There are many weird and wonderful things to behold on the Prairies.

Back in 2018, when we launched *Parallel Prairies: Stories of Manitoba Speculative Fiction*, we expressed surprise and gratitude at the sheer number of genre fiction writers who contributed to the project. It proved to be such a success that we always knew we should take the spotlight we had cast on Manitoba and shine it on the whole region.

There were plenty of great writers across the sweeping expanses of Alberta, Saskatchewan, and Manitoba, and more still who hailed from there, but had travelled elsewhere. Once again, we were thrilled to receive many great submissions, out of which we have selected the best, for your reading enjoyment, in this spiritual successor to *Parallel Prairies*.

These authors have called upon their experience to portray the Prairies as only they can, offering images of a sun-blasted Alberta in the throes of severe climate change; diabolic geese in northern Saskatchewan, flying high to spot the damned from a bird's-eye perspective; and gruesome horror "movies" which seem entirely too real and too familiar to the watcher, pulled from the dregs of a Winnipeg flea-market's offerings, along with many more.

We are also not unfamiliar with the lands to the west of us: Adam was born, and spent his early childhood, in Edmonton; Darren is Manitoba-born, but began his journalism career in the Alberta badlands, reporting out of Drumheller. Like many of the writers in this collection, we have had the opportunity to experience and enjoy these flatlands—and be inspired by them.

We are pleased and privileged to have the opportunity to share these writers' work with you, the reader. Many of them may be known to you already, and if they aren't, we hope this anthology is the gateway that leads you to check out their other works.

The writers who call the Prairie home have not been just colleagues, or friends, but inspirations for us. We hope they'll be the same to you, too. Happy reading.

DARREN RIDGLEY AND ADAM PETRASH
EDITORS

EGGSHELLS

Linda Trinh

I noticed her first. The scent of lotus blossoms and green mangoes, sweet yet sharp, announced her presence. Her vibrations were those of a stream chuckling as it trickled to a riverbed: hope and possibility. I stepped back, shifting away from her intensity, as if physical waves were pushing me backward. As far as I knew, I was alone in my ability to sense what I did.

What would happen if I strolled right up to her, chest out and chin up, and just asked her for her number? Could I lace her long fingers through my own?

The Forks was busy this Saturday afternoon; everyone excited to venture out after long days of prairie darkness spent indoors. Some days, Winnipeg was colder than the surface of Mars, gripped in a deep freeze where the wind chill made it feel like below 50 degrees Celsius. Today, the sun was cheerful, glinting off the packed snow. I heard the churning of the earth on its axis, easing into evening, and I sensed the spiciness of the coming equinox on the wind.

She swung around and looked back in my direction, the grace of a dancer apparent in the line of her shoulders, her back, the turn-out of her ankles. She looked right at my charm suspended in the air in front of her. She took a step forward, plucked my charm from its spot and slipped it under her white parka. She turned around and walked the other way, melting into the crowd.

The object I considered my charm was a shard the size of my palm that glowed amber, iridescent. It was smooth and slightly concave on the inside and grainy like the surface of a newly repaired tooth on the outside. It reminded me of a broken piece of pottery with its random shape and sharp edges. A soft and constant hum radiated from it and the scent of damp mountain rock and moss mingling with seawater tickled the inside of my nose. The object was usually invisible to everyone but me. Sometimes, people looked back quickly, confusion knitted between their brows, trying to decipher what was there. These were usually people on whom I sensed chrysanthemum and reed flute. They quickly passed by before I could burst over to them. Did you sense it? Are you like me?

When I felt lonely or fretful, I came here to be with my charm, like when people sit in the park or visit an art gallery. I was compelled to come here. This winter was especially hard, with Bà Nội passing away and Hélène moving out.

"I can't do this anymore Hùng. I love you… but… all of it… it's too much…" Hélène said as she was sorting through the mugs, taking the set of six plain white ones and leaving behind "I ❤ NY," "Coffee, then good morning," and the one with the picture of the two of us with Santa that I had given her as a gift.

It took so much out of me to take the bus downtown to be with my charm. I bathed in its energy until my sobs quieted, until I was able to eat congee with soy sauce without throwing up, until the feeling of myself returned to me.

I was already a few beats behind her when my legs started to work again.

She was so quick with the theft. So brazen.

I caught up to her as she walked past the Canadian Museum for Human Rights, my high-heeled boots crunching on the salted sidewalk.

"Hey, what are you doing with that?" I pointed to my charm, now in her hands. Its hum had changed, had become incessant, annoyed, and the scent of seawater on wet rock became overwhelming.

She raised her eyebrows. "You can see this?"

I nodded. Standing next to her was like wading through a pond of fuchsia lotus under a starry sky.

Her alarm turned into interest. "Người Việt?"

"My dad's Vietnamese." I replied in English.

"But you were born here?"

"A little personal. Like first date material." I put my hands in my pocket. "My question?"

"They'll come looking for you too." She tucked her arm under mine and began walking again. "Let's go."

"This isn't the way to ask me out, you know." But I didn't remove her arm. The scent of her loose locks blowing in the wind reminded me of dipping slices of green mango in a sauce of sugar and nước mắm. I giggled.

She began to run as we travelled a few blocks away to the Exchange District, dragging me with her. The sun was low, caressed by dusty pink skies. I breathed in the frost.

"They may not have noticed it's missing yet." She kept stopping and looking behind her. "We were quick. But we need to keep going."

I liked how she referred to me and her as a *we.* I never thought to ask—who are they or why are we running from them? I was so dazzled by her I suspended my natural curiosity.

I stumbled into a pothole, twisting my right ankle, and I screamed out. "Let me catch my breath." I reached down to rub my ankle. It was hard to regulate my breathing, like being stuck in a vacuum.

She held my hand to steady me. We were both without gloves. A warmth like drinking hot tea after a long walk from the bus stop flowed through my bloodstream and I no longer felt so terrible. I missed the feeling of holding hands with someone, running my thumb along theirs, and squeezing their palm, knowing I was in the world.

"Where we going?" I finally thought to ask as we began running again. I smelled smoke, like a match being lit, bitter in my mouth.

"We just need to get as far away from where we were as soon as possible." She looked back. "Before they come."

My ears rang with a high-pitched noise, and I put my hands over them as a reflex, knowing that it wouldn't help anything. I just needed to do something. It stopped—a pause, a breath—then started again, a regular pulsing of vibrations.

She heard it too, stopping suddenly and ducking into an arched alleyway that was a popular spot for wedding pictures. It was deserted today. She pulled my charm from her jacket pocket. Its sea-breeze fragrance had deepened into the brininess of a hurricane and it no longer hummed. She dropped it into the grey snow like it had seared her skin.

"They found us." Her voice was frantic. "They're going to destroy it." She was pacing, overwhelmed.

The sound of the pulsing sped up. It sounded more like thunder now, erratic crackling in the air.

"Close your eyes," she said.

"What?" I could barely hear her through all the clamour.

"Close your eyes. Close them," she screamed, her energy barely contained within her own body. "If we don't look upon them, they may spare us." She closed her eyes and flattened herself against the wall.

I closed my eyes.

I smelled smoke again but it had changed. Charred. Burnt. A forest fire raging.

The pulsing sped up again. The volume amplified. I envisioned loops of the sound waves so tightly squished, they almost merged all together.

I tasted bitter smoke at the back of my throat, burning the inside of my nose. Building and building until I could barely breathe.

Then it stopped.

An absence of anything.

I opened my eyes and saw an indent in the snow where my charm used to be. I imagined space aliens blasting it with their radar guns before beaming back to their spaceships.

My chest tightened and I clenched my fists. I mourned the loss of my charm, an emptiness in me where it once held a space.

Tears streaked her face. "The Dragon and the Fairy weep this day." She dropped to her knees and looked past me into the chilly air.

I wanted to take her pain away. I hated anyone in pain. That was what made me an ineffective counsellor: I felt the need to fix things for everyone. Hélène had said I held on too tightly, tried too hard, not wanting anyone to leave.

I put my left hand on her shoulder and she winced, pulling away.

"Sorry. Habit." I said as I clasped my hands in front of me.

She rubbed her shoulder where I had touched her and looked down at my hands. She stared at me as if for the first time, her eyes like crystals. "It's getting dark." She looked at the setting sun. "Meet me tomorrow?" She rose to her feet.

"Wait, tell me what that was," I said. She seemed to know more about my charm than I did.

"It's a piece of eggshell." She watched me.

I stared at her.

She continued, "A piece of eggshell left behind by our ancestors, from the eggs they hatched from."

"The fairy and the dragon?" I asked.

She nodded. "I must go. Nothing good happens after dark. Noon tomorrow. The phở place close to Health Sciences Centre."

"Wait. Don't go." Panic tingled in my ears. I didn't want to be alone after she had stepped into my life, or more like, after I went chasing after her. "What's your name? I'm Hùng,"

"Hiền." She walked away.

"It's a date!" I called after her, my heart beating quickly.

○

In bed, I dreamed about Bà Nội, her silvery grey hair curling around her neck, minty medicinal green ointment and clinking ceramic teacups. Dad had inherited her small nose and easy laugh and passed them down to me, so everyone said. When I was a kid, Bà Nội had hummed to me as she swung me on a hammock for afternoon naps when Dad was working and Mom had already left us.

Bà Nội was the one who told me we came from the union of the Dragon King Lạc Long Quân of the seas and the Fairy Goddess Âu Cơ of the mountains. The Fairy Goddess laid a large sac that contained one hundred eggs. One hundred babies hatched from these eggs. The couple was happy, for a while. Yet she ached for the glittering mountaintops and he longed to be reunited with the seas. When they parted ways, fifty children went with their mother to the mountains where they became the highlanders. Fifty children went with their father to the seashore where they became the first kings of the land.

As a kid hearing this story, I had imagined all the eggs breathing as one, soft and leathery shells like reptilian eggs. The babies slipped free of the bright white shells, casting off their layer of protection, born into this world.

The next morning, I was surprised to wake up without the crushing weight of anxiety, no longer smelling the bitter dark tea of monotony. Meeting Hiền sparked something within me. For the first time in a long time, I was excited to start the day. I felt more like myself again. I took care, wearing eyeliner, mascara, and lip gloss, a bulky silver tunic over black tights and knee-high boots. I even curled my shoulder-length hair in loose ringlets.

At lunch with Hiền, I ordered the phở tái bò viên and sinh

tố xoài. I asked for extra noodles and extra lime for the soup. The smoothie was a bit too sweet, but I could tell by the flavour that they used fresh mango and not the powder.

Hiền got the bún bò xào and her long fingers were like those of a knitter as she poured in her nước mắm and tossed everything together with her plastic chopsticks—vermicelli noodles, egg rolls, pan fried beef, peanuts, bean sprouts, and herbs. She was still the sound of water flowing and the scent of fruit and flowers.

I took a deep breath, pretending to smell the phở broth, but really trying to get hints of her scent through the star anise and lime of my soup.

"Why do you have a boy's name?" she asked.

I shrugged. "Dad wanted a son."

She ate a piece of beef. "My name is gentle. I'd rather have yours—brave, hero."

I smiled, pleased. "So the eggshells? I thought it was all a myth."

"Well, it isn't. After the eggs hatched and the children of the Fairy and the Dragon emerged, something extraordinary happened. The eggshell fragments embedded into our people and they were passed along through the generations. As our ancestors went all over the world, they transported those fragments." She added more nước mắm to her bowl. "As the boat people came to Canada, they carried the eggshells with them. Some of those eggshells dislodged and anchored themselves to other things and stayed in various places."

"Why would the eggshells do that?" I took a sip of my sinh tố.

She lifted her arms and pointed her fists skyward, "Only the Fairy and the Dragon know. Perhaps it's a remembrance of our homeland. A beacon to the past. A bit of the ancestors in a new place we call home." She raised her eyebrows at me. "How long have you been able to sense it?"

"Always. It called to me. A beacon. That's a good word. Never met anyone else who was like me before," I said.

"So you know more than I do why the eggshells anchor in a place."

"Why'd you steal it then?" I was only half joking.

"I wasn't stealing it. I was saving it." She raised her voice but quickly lowered it again. "Trying to anyways. I've been trying to save eggshells for years now."

"From who?" I put down my chopsticks.

"From those who would wish us harm. Those who want us to forget our culture, erase our connection to our past."

"So this is what you do? You're a saviour?" I asked.

"I don't want them to disappear. I don't want us to lose more than we have already. But I failed yesterday, again."

She looked so forlorn. I wanted to kiss her then and chase away the sadness. She was a garden in full bloom drenched in sunlight. I just wanted to see her smile. "I know where there's another eggshell."

She reached across the glass-top table and held out her hand. I put mine in hers, again feeling her light and warmth through my veins.

"Will you take me? We can save it together," she said.

I nodded, swept up in her.

○

We walked the trails behind Assiniboine Forest along Grant Avenue. Snowflakes, wet and heavy, were twirling and tumbling down, the kind that clung to eyelashes and soaked woolen coats. Winter was not leaving without one last storm.

"Are we close?" She held my hand, following ever so slightly behind me.

I nodded. "Over here. Found it during the summertime. My ex and I were riding our bikes. The clanging from the charm—I mean the eggshell—surprised me. I almost fell off."

"What does it sound like to you?" She wiped the snowflakes off her cheeks.

I looked up at the sky, now dense with clouds, deciding on an answer. "Chattering, like a trilling, a purring."

"Like it was speaking to you."

I smiled at her and wanted so much to embrace her, to hold within me her babbling brook. I wanted to suspend this moment, to clasp tight this feeling.

"Just here." I pointed.

Embedded within the exposed root of a Manitoba maple tree, the eggshell was the size of a loonie, almost covered now by the dusting of snow. It trilled to its own melody and held the scent of sea salt breeze like my charm before it.

Hiền knelt and wiped away the snow, revealing the entire piece.

I felt a tingling within and almost buckled over. I felt the same breathlessness I had yesterday when we were running through the Exchange District, when the other eggshell was destroyed.

She put two fingers around the eggshell and began to twist it, attempting to loosen it from the root.

I heard a high-pitched sound. And it began to pulse at regular intervals.

"Wait." I took a step back. I began to realize something. The eggshell had only begun to protest when we tried to move it. "Hiền, how many have you collected? Like, how many of them haven't been destroyed."

She didn't look at me. "They've all been destroyed. But not this one."

I shuddered. "How do you know?"

The pulsing began to speed up.

But she was no longer focused on me. There was a shift in her. Or maybe I was sensing her for who she really was for the first time. Her scent soured, not the freshness and tartness of green mango, but mango that had rotted, become putrid and too far gone. The chuckling stream was more of an incessant rushing river. The veil was lifted. I was no longer dazzled.

Unshed tears pooled at the corners of my eyes mixed with the falling flakes. The snowfall was getting heavier.

"I don't think you should take it," I whispered.

She yanked on it with so much force, she fell backwards, the eggshell between her fingers.

The pulsing changed again and was now like crackling thunder. Smoke and flame filled my nostrils. Like before in the Exchange District.

"They're coming. I thought we would have more time." She stood up and held the eggshell in her right palm. "Let's get out of here. Hurry before they come and the eggshell is destroyed." She was looking past me, perhaps past time and space itself.

"Put it back Hiền. Don't you get it?" I stood in front of her.

Her eyes were glassy.

I cupped her face in my hands. I brought my mouth to her ear, "You're creating what you think is chasing you."

She pulled away and held the eggshell close to her chest.

I took a step toward her. "You're destroying them."

"No." She shook her head. "I am saving them." She closed her eyes. "No, no."

"Can't take them." I now sensed something I didn't understand before, when I was still enchanted by her. "The eggshells go where they go, the spaces they need to be. Like you said, they go to the places we call home."

I reached for the eggshell in her hand. She swatted my arm away.

She held it. "No, that's not true. It's not. This is what I must do, need to do. I need what they are. Without them, who am I? And this time is different. It's the first time I collected two at the same time, in one spot." She had to shout over the sound of the pulses. "This one, and..."

I knew it before she said it.

"Me," I whispered.

"You," she screamed.

For a moment, I registered nothing, suspended.

"When did you know?" I asked after what seemed like a long stretch of nothing.

"When we met. When you touched my shoulder after the other eggshell was destroyed. Didn't you ever wonder why you could sense them?" she asked.

When she said it, I knew. Perhaps I had always known. They were calling to me, blood to blood, ancestor to descendant. I looked down at my hands. For the first time, I saw on my left hand a sliver of eggshell rooted in the fingernail of my middle finger, glimmering amber. How could I have never sensed it before, looking at my hands every day? I had never expected it, never expected to be more than ordinary. Now it was so clear. A gentle hum and the scent of sea salt dancing on a mountain cliff.

"I must save them both." She grabbed my hand. "I must have it."

I saw in her eyes a reflection of what I had seen in my mirror on the days I was weighed down with longing and emptiness. I wouldn't wish that feeling on her or anyone.

She clawed at my fingernail, gentle at first and then desperately.

I didn't try to pull my hand away.

She shouted above the pulsing. "I can't take it. I can't grab onto it." There was a thinness in her voice and she began to cry.

I knew what I should do. I hated anyone in pain. This I could fix. "For you." I pulled the eggshell from my fingernail and placed it in her own. I didn't know what this would mean for me, if I would still sense what I did. I was willing to risk that.

It melded to her fingernail. Hiền dropped our hands and held her face up to the sky, snowflakes melting on her skin and washing away her tears.

I took the loonie-sized eggshell from her and placed it back into the tree root. The pulsing stopped. The scent of burning bush dissolved. The eggshell melted into the tree and vanished, ready to re-appear when it was needed.

The snow glittered under the rising gibbous moon. The flakes fell without sound and the air held its breath.

THE SLOUGH

Sheryl Normandeau

Anyone who grows up on the Alberta prairie knows you don't go messing around near the farm slough. You can't get two weeks into summer without hearing about some stupid kid drowning, and statistically speaking, at least 6.258 of the little monsters break through the ice and die every winter, too. But we farmers put up with the dying, because slough water is the lifeblood of our crops, our livestock, and our homes.

Well, for some folk, maybe. Our slough is a stinkhole, with water like pitch. It oozes so much filth and decay that even the blackflies leave it alone. On hot, sticky days in July, when the air is still, the stench carries a sweet half mile clear up to the house.

Nobody seems to know how long the slough had been there. It had been a fixture on the land when my great-granddad bought the property in 1907, from a Polish immigrant who didn't speak a lick of English. Great-granddad apparently took one look at the dank hole and decided he'd rather pump out the farm's irrigation water from nearby Bullpound Creek. My great-great uncle Philip dug our well in the summer of 1915, and the water ran clear and clean and plentiful. Always has, until the past year or so. You can't draw water for three generations and expect it to keep producing forever. Still, it could have waited until after I was gone—there isn't anyone after me to need it.

My first recollection of the slough's particular peculiarities came the summer I was seven. I couldn't do enough to get out of my mother's way. My dad had buggered off with some floozy from Hanna, leaving my mother and me stuck out at the farm. Granddad never liked my dad; said he was no good as a farmer, and a worse husband than that. Along the road that led to the dissolution of their marriage, my parents had moved onto the farm when I was in diapers.

"I was desperate," Granddad said to me many years later as we sat on the porch one afternoon.

His mouth contorted around the wad of mud-brown tobacco he always chewed. "I needed your mother here," he said, and I looked away like any man should when his grandfather's eyes are misting over with tears. "I couldn't handle your grandmother anymore and your dad, even though he was a stupid son of a gun, was an extra body on a tractor."

Mother had some grand scheme of moving to town herself, but I think everyone knew she wouldn't leave Granddad alone after the Alzheimer's had taken Grandma.

So, there I was. I scrambled out of bed at six every morning, even though I was on summer vacation, and was out the door and finished my chores well before Mother crawled out of her room and started the day's drinking. Most times, Granddad was already on the fields—I could just make out the hump of the old green tractor in the distance. We kept chickens, pigs, horses, and a few dairy cows at the time, and once I had fed them all, I grabbed my fishing pole and headed off to the creek to see if the 'bows were biting. Those quiet summer mornings were good times for me, a respite from all the bullies and the saints in my life, everyone trying to either hinder or help me. I was a weird, gangly kid who didn't fit in with the crowd at school and was estranged from a family who seemed like they'd rather I didn't exist. My teachers, knowing my troubles at home, tried too hard to give me reasons to thrive despite my situation. I didn't take too well to their attempts and shrank away, which only validated my status as a loser.

One morning in late June, I wandered down to the slough. I don't know why, but I felt like I should head over there. Granddad was tinkering on a stall latch in the stable and I didn't tell him where I was going. I guess I had some notion that I would find some frogs for bait, but at the same time, I knew I would come up empty. Nothing lived near the slough. Nothing lived *in* the slough.

Still I went down there.

The rank odour that usually emanated from the water was remarkably subdued that morning—maybe the wind was blowing just the right way or my nose was just so used to it that the stench didn't clog up the olfactory glands any more. The black water sat as still as an oil slick below me as I crested the rise and stared down. I wondered if the water was like the quicksand I had seen the gang fight their way out of on a recent episode of my favourite TV show. I didn't intend to test it out, possessing neither a magical rope, nor a group of clever, resourceful—and most importantly, loyal—friends who would do anything to save me, but for some reason, I started down towards the slough anyway. My cheap vinyl sneakers popped out squelching noises that reminded me, happily, of farts.

Suddenly I found myself with my right foot in the slough and Granddad was yanking my arm, tearing me up so violently that my shoe fell off. How he got there so fast I can't calculate. He shoved me to the ground, and I looked up at him, dazed, my eyes filled with tears. My foot felt like I had stuck it in the wood stove; I looked down and the woolen fibres of my sock were covered in black, molten goo. I began to wail, and Granddad reached down and tore the sock away.

"You stupid, boy?" Granddad hollered. His face was purple and I was near hysterics. Granddad stood there for a long moment, looking down at me, his only grandson, the idiot. Then he did something so uncharacteristic it shocked me more than nearly being sucked down into the slough. He plunked heavily down on the bank and put his arm around me, gripping me so tightly I whimpered. "I'm going to tell you a story," he said.

I nodded meekly, trying hard to stifle the hiccupping my crying had spawned.

"Okay," Granddad said. "My story is about this here slough and a boy named Timmy. Now, you mind all this, 'cause it's the honest-to-God truth, and maybe if you hear it straight, the same thing won't happen to you.

"You understand why this slough is bad, right? Not just because you could drown in it."

He paused and licked his lips like he was needing a good stiff drink.

"It's because a demon lives in it."

"What?" I blurted.

"No one knows its true name, but it has been living in the slough for as long as time has been ticking, way before any of us were born. Before the dinosaurs, like." Granddad took a deep breath. "It eats stupid little kids and other people who go near the slough. My friend Timmy was one of them.

"You see, the creature demands sacrifices. You know what that word means, boy? Sacrifice? It means you have to give up something big to get some sort of reward. The demon eats people so that the water flows and the crops grow. I know it doesn't make much sense to you, but if that thing in the slough is starving, then so are we. And our neighbours, too."

Questions exploded in my brain, but I clamped my teeth down behind my lips.

"Timmy was my friend when I was ten," he said finally. "The greatest bud a guy could ask for. We were always doing crazy stuff. That summer was the best of my life, until Timmy decided one day that we'd fire rocks into the slough with our slingshots.

"I knew we weren't supposed to go out there, but I didn't want to look like some little chickenshit to Timmy, so I grabbed my slingshot and some ammo and we headed over.

"It was fun, for a while—we lobbed a bunch of stones into the black mud and watched them slowly sink. Timmy could shoot way farther than I ever could, so after getting my butt handed to me over and over, I got tired and plopped down on the bank for a bit of a breather. It was a real scorcher out that day, so I took off my shirt and balled it up for a pillow and just lay there, looking up at the sky."

Granddad paused. "It was kind of like today," he said. "Hot and still, like you know something's going on."

I couldn't stop wriggling in anticipation. Strangely, my teeth were chattering. I suppose I was in shock.

"Timmy kept right on firing stones into the slough, whooping it up loudly for my benefit. I wouldn't have any of it and I guess I dozed off somehow. The next thing I knew, there was a weird noise, the gargle of an animal with a slit throat. My heart started hammering and I looked around frantically. Timmy was nowhere to be seen. I thought he'd gone off and hid just to bug me, but then I noticed this commotion out in the slough.

"There was Timmy, half-submerged, flailing wildly, his hair and face and arms dripping with black ooze. He was roiling around like jam in a kettle on a hot stove and I could see the blood spurting as the demon sliced him open. He made a noise, a sound like I've never heard since."

Granddad fumbled for a pinch of tobacco from his pouch. He didn't look at me. "I'm not proud of this," he said. "All I could do was holler. I was too scared to move and help my best friend while he was getting savaged.

"By the time my parents got to us, Timmy was gone. The creature had devoured him. I told them about the demon, but no one believed me. Timmy had drowned, they said. I now know they were lying to keep me from going crazy."

Granddad sighed. "I was sent away to a hospital in Calgary for a few months after that, to get rid of the nightmares. But I heard the stories: Timmy wasn't the only one sacrificed to the demon. The old guy who owned the land before us lost his first daughter. And there are legends that go back even before then, from the tribes that passed through before the European settlers came. Mark my words, boy, you were almost another."

I shivered in the heat. I was suddenly running a fever.

○

Let me tell you something in confidence. I didn't speak of this to any of those doctors that stitched me up last night in the hospital—they would have put me in the loony bin for sure. I told them I had an accident on the farm. They know something isn't quite right about that story, but so far no one has said anything.

I went down to the slough last night, just before dusk. I hadn't left the house in a few weeks. It's a good thing I sold the livestock a couple of years ago, or they would have been hooped. Mrs. Hamley from down the road had been leaving home-cooked casseroles on the porch, but even though I ate them, I couldn't figure out the reason for her charity. Not like I have ever done the Hamleys a turn and there she was, trying to keep this one bitter soul a-flickering even though she and her old man don't have a penny between them.

I squinted out at the fields. A brown haze of dust particles banded the horizon. The air seemed desperately hot, sucking moisture from my skin. There had been no rain for two months; before that, a brief snowstorm had yielded the merest skiff of flakes as dry as salt. The earth had lain bare all winter, while the frigid winds howled and blasted the topsoil against the house, seaming it into the chinks of the outbuildings. It was the third year in a row that I had seeded and the grain had refused to germinate. The

Hamleys and the Transoms to the north and the Austins west of the creek were in the same boat, every one of us sitting on acres of parched ground and shrivelled seed.

Ashes to ashes, dust to dust.

I guess I could say it was the perfect reflection of my life. I had never done well for myself. When those amped-up Bible-thumpers back in town rumble about how everyone is just a speck in God's eye, I guess I am the smallest one of all. I can't speak for the rest of those poor buggers out there, but we all get what we deserve, right?

I could hear Granddad's voice: *The demon eats people so that the water flows and the crops grow.*

I still didn't want to believe him. Crops grow because of rain, sunlight, air, soil. Not because some demon in a slough permits it.

I couldn't help but think about how it all comes around. Here I stood again on that rise, like I had forty-one years ago, when frogs and quicksand were on my mind.

Only now the slough was empty.

I blinked; knuckled my eyes. In the hundred and fifteen years my family had farmed this land, the slough had never once dried up. Now the black ooze had completely receded, and the gaping pit was rimmed with minerals. Although some juvenile part of me had always wondered if Granddad's story about Timmy had any inkling of truth, there was no doubt now that the old fart had been lying, telling me nonsense just so I wouldn't drown in the mud. Of course, that didn't quite explain the searing pain I had felt in my foot that day, but when you're a kid, you watch too much TV and your imagination runs wild. The slough was just a big hole in the ground like any other, a vessel for groundwater and rain.

I started laughing until tears sprang to my eyes. I stood there for a minute, blubbering, and then I took my boots and socks off and walked straight down the banks of the slough.

The slope was high and ridged and went down maybe forty, fifty feet. But my footing was sure and steady.

Warm crumbles of crystalline dirt split off between my toes, gritting the soft skin of my feet. I held my arms scarecrow-wide. The air was perfectly still, no wind kissing the hair on my forearms or whispering at my neck. No birds or insects flew. No cloud moved, nor burst wide open to warn of the pending apocalypse.

"What do you say to this, Granddad?" I hissed gleefully to the sky.

Okay, so cockiness doesn't look good on me, and I guess I deserved it for taunting the dead. Because the second I stepped down on the flat bed of the slough, all hell broke loose. For real.

This is the stuff I didn't tell the doctors and the nurses.

I mean, what would they think if I said that a glob of black oily ooze with teeth as big as a combine's and claws that could drive through a herd of cattle like they were cubes of meat on a giant shish-kebab grabbed me and tried to pull me *under* the dirt of a dry slough? What if I had told them that the reason I was now missing six of my previously well-preserved ten toes was because the blazing breath of the black demon's maw singed them clear off? Or that while I shrieked like a wounded coyote and scrabbled back up the bank of the slough, bleeding from open wounds, the savage creature filled my ears with its keening hunger, with its desire for blood.

"SAVE," it whined as it scraped a claw down my right leg, splitting the denim of my jeans and separating muscle and tendon from bone like the most skillful surgeon.

"GIVE," it demanded, and despite my fear I understood just how starving and weak it was. It had been a long time since Timmy had died.

"FEED."

The demon's tongue lashed at my back, and my shirt melted, fusing to my skin. All I could see was white sky. The top of the bank seemed impossible to reach without bleeding or burning to death first.

As I lay in my hospital bed, I thought of Mrs. Hamley and her Kindness Casseroles, and of the Transoms and the Austins, all of them ready to pack it in and head for the bright lights of Calgary. I thought of the well running dry, of the creek where I used to fish now a waterless trough for smooth stones. I thought of the seeds in the earth, lying dormant forever. And I thought of my bachelorhood, of the children I would never hold, and the emptiness of the old farmhouse where my family has lived for more than a century. *You have to give up something big to get some sort of reward.* Well, Granddad, it took me way longer than it should have, but I finally see that you're right.

Yeah, I know. I'm one seriously lucky bastard. Sure, I'm predominately toeless, burned, mangled, bruised, fractured, and torn, but I'm alive. And I'll lay money on this: once I hobble back home, I'll notice a trickle—the slightest dribble—of water in the creek, in the well, and in the slough.

I only hope I've given enough.

THE GOOD GIRLS

S.M. Beiko

"Everything is a bit strange in this house," Betty said from the library sofa, her rustling figure cast in the oddments of frayed dusk light. She had thin hair and no eyes, and every day her rotting skin rotted more.

"Please stop," Sandy asked, meek as a mouse, hands covering her ears—but her eyes, no, she mustn't look away. She knew the rules. She was a good girl, after all.

Betty sighed, crossing one broken leg over what was left of the other, the meat dangling, the bones splintered, like a cruel hammer had been there first.

"You're quiet. That's good," Betty said. "Sometimes it's better to see horror now, to take it in." Betty's lips stretched in what could have been a smile, but it was getting darker, getting harder to see. Something plinked on the hardwood below the sofa. Probably Betty's teeth.

"It's good I'm here now, to show you."

○

Sandy perched on the swing outside, in the huge, overgrown garden looking out into a thin treeline of Manitoba maples. Her black leather shoes with the shining buckles scraped in the dirt. Her mother had taken to calling her sullen, a word Sandy didn't know then, but she knew it now, due to the obliging dictionary in her father's rarely-occupied study.

It wasn't that she was sullen about any one thing. It was a

lot of things. The cross words her father blurted. His yawning absences. Her mother's unspoken misery.

And Betty was not going anywhere anytime soon, as her continued sundown visits proved. But Sandy, if anything, was clever. She may have been quiet. She may have kept her curiosities to herself, most times, dreading their results.

But Sandy was patient. So she listened.

"They mean well," Betty said from the swing beside her. Sandy looked up like a dog with its ears pricked forward. Behind the swings, a distance off, was the kitchen window, through which Sandy knew her mother was watching her, studying her, trying to figure out what was wrong with her child. If only Sandy could turn, dart her eyes, and perhaps the alchemy of motherhood, that keen sense of knowing what Sandy had done wrong before she'd done it, would have saved her.

The swing creaked. Betty must have pushed off with her mouldering foot, canted unnaturally inward, to get some momentum. She swung, floating, like a discarded plastic bag.

"I'd kill for a smoke," she said. Then she laughed. Then she sighed. The sound was a grunt of air through a frozen wasps' nest. "Listen. It's going to get harder. You're young now, you can't see so far in front of you. But it's best I talk to you like you're old enough to know better."

The swing set continued to creak as they swung. "You're quiet. That's good for protecting yourself. But it doesn't do much good for protecting anyone else. You'll need to find your voice sometime. You'll find your voice that much quicker with this next rule: don't tell your mother. Don't blame her, either. Like I said, she means well. Mine did, too, all the way to the Laundry, and I trusted her, did as I was told. But it wasn't enough. It still isn't, even though times have changed, I'd think. I may not have eyes, but I can still see the world. Seventy years later, nothing much has changed in it."

Sandy heard the vertebrae in the meat of Betty's neck clicking with the effort as Betty turned her face to Sandy, with what was left of said face sloughing off with every minute spent above ground. Sandy imagined, for a moment, that such a ghoulish face might have been lovely once. Sandy could see the white of Betty's skull.

"The power of a girl is everything. They will try to take it from you. But they are afraid of it. They try to push it down, to make you swallow it, and they are used to getting their way. But never give up that power. Even after you've lost yourself. Never lose your voice, even when there is no one to hear it."

For the first time since Betty arrived, Sandy took stock of her heartbeat. Its slow beating. Her utter calm. She was not scared right now. She had chosen not to be.

"What's it like to die?" Sandy asked.

Betty was still, her skeleton and remaining flesh moved only by the wind passing through the prairie property. Since her eye sockets were empty, and most of the skin around her mouth was gone, Sandy realized she could've been thinking anything.

Betty's head creaked forward, west, to the setting sun, and Sandy knew it was okay now to look away.

"Dunno, but. Best thing I ever did."

○

Sandy's mother used different words after that. Disobedient. Difficult. Wilful. Sandy knew these words, but she wasn't scared of them, either. Not anymore.

"What's gotten into you?" her father asked after her mother had recounted Sandy's wandering from the house at night, coming home, the hem of her nightdress stained with red prairie soil, her fingernails full of it, baby-knuckle skin ravaged with cuts. Never mind what she had been doing, where she'd been scrabbling.

All of that was secondary to the same tired warning Sandy, and every girl before her, had been given, but never offered a solution to: "Don't you know it's not safe out after dark for a little girl?"

"I know," Sandy answered immediately.

What startled her parents most were her shining eyes, meeting theirs, measuring them.

"I am learning."

○

Betty taught Sandy about the others in the house.

"They're just tired," Betty said. "They want to be here less than you do."

There was the stretched washerwoman, wrapped around the plumbing, moaning whenever the hot water tank went on to feed the washing machine. The harried farm wife whose tongue had been cut out, and so tapped against the windowpane in her own sullen code. The maiden who sorted through the ashes of the fireplace, looking for the letter that had been burned there hundreds of years before, face blackened by smoke. This house was an old one, on the edge of several Assiniboia river lots now being redeveloped. It had a history, and so did the faint outlines of the women left behind. They all looked up at Sandy but didn't say a word.

Betty said, "They just want to go home."

"But aren't they home already?" Sandy asked.

She felt fiercely protective of each wispy horror, each haint she had found, carefully cataloging each one throughout the enormous house. And though Betty warned her not to treat them as pets, Sandy felt sorry for them.

"No," Betty answered, so quickly and harshly that Sandy remembered to be afraid. Then Betty's broken jaw softened, the mandible falling askew like a busted piano plunger. Sandy reached out and gently hooked it back into place.

Once again, Betty was very still. Her voice was impossibly soft and alive. "Not home yet."

○

Sandy grew up in that house and all its archived memory of pain. Her parents stopped noticing her nighttime rambles—or perhaps they didn't want to know about them.

Sandy remained quiet.

But she listened harder.

She went into the night and accounted for all the things out there that could snatch her and do her harm, but each one she looked dead in the eye, and they always turned away, afraid and unsure why. And Sandy liked it.

Her parents fought every night. They were loud. And when they weren't, the undercurrent of violence in the quiet was deafening. At breakfast, her mother would look up at Sandy and quickly look away. The haints shook their grotesque heads. Sandy watched her mother, mouth closed so tight it might have been sewn that way, and though Betty had been gone a long time by then, her words were incised across Sandy's skull. She believed if the flesh of her scalp were ever to fall away, the words would be there in neat printing: Never lose your voice.

Sandy's father struck her mother only once for Sandy to find hers.

○

As she got older, Sandy traded her filthy nightgown for the proper togs. Steel-toed boots. A good shovel. Betty had told her where to dig, since she'd been in the ground a very long time, and in a centuries-old town with a penchant for silence, for turning away from the horrors that happened next door, the dead had nothing better to do than talk.

"Can't do much of the labour myself," Betty had said, holding up her rattling hands. "That's why I came to find you. This house isn't particularly special. Crimes and sadness and misery and harm don't follow specific rules to lay down roots. But it was my house, once." She gestured to the haints. "It was theirs, too. And it's been long enough. Soon as I heard you were moving in, I'd had it. We all had. No more good girls going to waste."

Betty was very forthright. Difficult. Sandy liked that. "You're small now but you'd be amazed what light work small hands can make." Then Betty wove her crumbling crunching dust-fingers into Sandy's. They held tight. They popped and disintegrated. "You'll know what to do. You're a good girl, through and through."

○

Sandy was going to make her father afraid.

Her mother slept on the couch that night. The washerwoman in the pipes was still, but Sandy knew she was listening. The woman against the window did not tap, but peered in, and when Sandy passed, the woman nodded. The girl at the fireplace did not bother with the ashes, her translucent hands folded in her lap.

Sandy left the front door open and went up the stairs.

The trick was in the eyes. The truth was that anyone could see anything you wanted them to, if you looked deep enough. Betty called it a sort of nearsightedness. That Sandy just happened to look the right way, to have the same misgivings, which was why she could see Betty and some others couldn't. Sandy had looked, and had never looked away, and had chosen not to be afraid.

Behind Sandy, the stairs creaked as footsteps joined hers. She did not need to look back this time. These women, the bodies of long-lost neighbours, had not been buried far away—after all, the best crimes are committed at home and buried there. You just had to know where to dig.

She continued to her parents' bedroom.

The other trick was knowing where to look, and when. Sandy's father looked at her more now, the older she got, the more her body changed. He looked freely and too long and it made Sandy's jaw tight, but though he looked, he did not see. Did not want to. He was busy looking elsewhere, comfortable in a house with a Divine history of pain, because it had nothing to do with him. Never mind that the house was inexpensive due to the recorded suffering that had happened here. "Good girls will do as they're told," he'd said to his wife and daughter.

In the bedroom, Sandy opened the door wide so the others could follow. She stood over her father's side of the bed, careful not to wake her mother, and she looked.

○

The hole was already dug. That was the easy part. Sandy had spent her nights practising, and this one had been so easy it was like it dug itself.

But her father had woken up when she'd dumped him in the hole, and he screamed. Sandy looked at him. He went very still.

"Honey," he said, and he kneeled, begging. "Be a good girl."

Sandy thought of Betty, her teeth clinking to the floor like a silver spoon on a champagne glass. It was time to find her voice. She smiled.

"Always, daddy."

Then she and the haints, whose bodies had come back to see this for themselves, who had helped carry him here with their rotting hands, filled in the hole together.

This was the first and last time Sandy's father had looked and truly seen, and his final screams were from the terror of suddenly knowing this coterie of dead women, and less from the dirt crushing him to darkness.

○

Sandy still lives in the house. The haints are long gone. New holes were dug, their spirits' bodies allowed to take back what had been left behind, to take those restless ghosts home, at last, in those crumbling bags of bones.

Betty was the first of the good girls Sandy had helped, before clearing out the others. Betty's departure had shown her the way that her father needed to take. Sandy remembers it often:

It took Sandy not long at all to find what Betty had come to her house looking for, when Sandy was so small and was only beginning to see. Betty's haint was in the attic. And though Sandy had searched the house high and low these many years, this haint had kept itself hidden. Had not even wanted her cursed body to find it. Sandy wondered if it was because the haint didn't wanted to get its hopes up.

But the haint was so quiet that it took another quiet girl to find her. She was as see-through and real as the others. Even in shadow, especially so, Betty was plain. She was lovely. Of course she had been dangerous to her own father, who had taken his liberties, and blamed it on her, and trapped her, until the last freedom death could afford.

"It's time to go home," Sandy said to Betty's haint, finally understanding. "It's time to see past this."

Betty walked away from Sandy that night, hand in hand with what was lost.

Though Sandy would never see Betty again, she saw others. Heard others. She pulled them out of the ground, with the strength in small hands she never imagined, and she put away back into those holes the men, too often men, that should no longer be seen, nor heard. As a good girl always should.

PURPLE CITY

Rhonda Parrish

It's just so cliché. That's what pisses me off the most. Like, does my entire life need to feel like it's been ripped from the pages of some stupid YA novel? Next thing you know I'll be learning to shoot a bow and volunteering as tribute.

I haven't seen Mom since the funeral. She stuck around for the first hour of the reception and then ducked into her room. My aunt Janice knocked to see if Mom wanted any of the million casseroles people had brought over, but Mom just shouted through the door that she wanted to be left alone.

As Janice was leaving, a pierogi casserole—which just happens to be my favourite—in each hand she said, "They happen in clusters, you know." That was it. "They happen in clusters, you know." And then she ducked out the door.

They happen in clusters. What am I supposed to do with that? Like, "Thanks for helping with our excess casserole problem by taking the only ones I like, Aunt Janice, but if you think your sister is going to kill herself maybe you could do something more than just hiss a warning at me?"

And it's not like Dad is going to be any help. As soon as we got home from the church he sunk into his recliner and the only time he's moved since is to get a fresh beer. Several fresh beers, actually.

He didn't even try to be social during the reception, left all that to me. He just sat in his chair and stared through people's legs at some soccer game on the television. And drank.

He's on his second six pack when Murphy sends me a text: *Want out?*

It's like she can read my damn mind.

So much, I reply. I look at Mom's closed door, conflicted for about a half a second before I make up my mind and add *Meet you in five.*

K, Murphy texts.

"I'm going out," I say to Dad, pulling on my favourite hoodie. It's dark blue with a bright orange Oilers logo on it. It used to be Korbin's, but when we broke up I kept it—I've never cared about hockey, but it's super comfy and looked better on me anyway.

Dad turns to look at me, then seems surprised we're the only two left in the room. Paper plates and plastic cups are scattered around on the flat surfaces, the only sign of all the people who'd been crowded into our living room just an hour before. "Everyone gone?"

"Yes." I resist the urge to say more, though the words are right there, waiting to come out.

"Where's your mother?"

I gesture toward their bedroom with my head.

Dad grunts and takes another drink from the bottle in his hand. I take that as consent, acknowledgement, whatever. I pull my shoes on and dip out the door before he can say anything to stop me.

It might be nice if he gave enough of a damn to want to, though.

Shoving that thought into the recesses of my mind, where it can linger in the shadows with so many others, I grab my bike from where it's been leaning against the side of the garage. The pedals get hung up with those of Jeremy's bike as I pull it away and it takes me several seconds to disentangle them. In the process his bike falls over. A lump forms in my throat, but I just leave the bike on the ground and walk mine overtop of it to leave the yard.

Another thought tries to force itself from the shadows of my mind but I hop on my bike and stuff it back down again.

It's getting dark when I reach Murphy at our spot halfway between our homes. Dead Cop Park, we usually call it, but I feel a little bit bad about that today. Maybe today I can think of it by its real name. I want to think of it by its real name. But I can't even remember what that is until I see it written on the sign.

"Hey," Murphy pedals over. The sound of her voice derails my guilt train about the park's name. Her hair is pulled into a loose French braid and she's wearing a big white turtleneck and jeans. Like always, she looks like she could have just walked off the pages of a magazine.

"Hey," I say.

"Fucked up day, eh?"

"Yeah. You don't even wanna know." She'd been at the funeral but hadn't come over for the reception. That was more of an adult thing.

I get off my bike and start to walk it beside her. We've been friends a long time. She's the one I called the day it happened, while the paramedics were still crowded into our house and crammed into Jeremy's room. I'd climbed into bed and called her from underneath the blankets, sobbing and gasping my way through the call, clinging to the sound of her voice in the darkness. Now I don't want to talk, nor do I want her to, and she seems to know that; to recognize it. Only the low hum of the traffic breaks the silence between us as we meander toward the Legislative Grounds. They aren't actually our destination, they just happen to be where we end up.

It's quieter there, insulated from the noise of traffic, and augmented with a handful of birds who haven't called it a day yet. Moths flutter around the lights, and small groups of people do the same. Most of them are looking at their phones and I suspect they're playing *Pokémon Go.* Jeremy and I used to come here to do that every now and then, too—when he could be bothered to spend time with his little sister, that is. Murphy never got into the game, though, so I leave my phone in my pocket.

As we walk between the Legislative building—the Ledge—and the big pool in the courtyard in front of it, all the fountains in the area are turned off. Their streams slowly collapse down and disappear, and it becomes even quieter without the white noise of running water. I hadn't noticed the sound until it was gone, but now in its absence the quiet is heavy.

"So," I say, trying to break the silence without actually having anything to say.

"So," she says back. Then she looks over at me and squishes her face up in a 'This is awkward' kind of expression.

I laugh and it feels both very wrong and very right; sort of how I felt laughing during Jeremy's eulogy. His basketball coach gave it, and he told the story about how Jeremy used to use his towel as a cape and run around the locker room in his underwear pretending to be Superman. It was so purely him that I couldn't help but laugh even while I was sitting in a church with his coffin. Lots of other people laughed, too—even Mom let out a watery chuckle—so I guess it was okay.

But then the unspoken question became, how does someone that exuberant, that full of life…

Nope. Not going there right now. I shove that down into the back of my mind with all the other shit I've been trying to avoid all day.

We walk our bikes around the corner of the Ledge, and then toward the back.

"Hey," Murphy says, pointing at one of the giant lights directed up at the building's walls. "Wanna turn on purple city?"

Neither one of us has ever done it before, but why not? It's not like I'm being the best conversationalist in the world so why not shift our perception a little bit.

"Sure," I say, but then nod to the couple making out right between the two big floodlights. "But maybe not here..."

"Maybe not," Murphy agrees, with a giggle.

We keep walking. There's a homeless man getting ready to sleep in the bushes near the west side so we go all the way around, returning to the front of the building. We pick the nearest floodlight and lean our bikes against the wall of the Ledge.

"So we just stare at it?" I ask.

"Into it, I think," Murphy says.

The light is huge, very bright and very orange. The idea behind Purple City is that if you stare into the orange floodlight long enough it temporarily burns out the parts of your eyes that detect that colour. Then, when you look away, you see everything in shades of purple.

"On three," Murphy says, and we both move to stand in front of the light. "One. Two. Three."

I look down, directly into the light as she says three. And immediately my eyes slam closed. It's a reflex, I can't help it—that light is *bright*.

I mutter a swear under my breath and force my eyes open again. Even though I'm not staring at anything but the light, shapes and shadows stir in front of my eyes. Blobbies and squiggles. And it hurts.

"How long do we need to stare at it?" I ask, blinking hard.

"I don't know."

"Count of ten?"

"Sure," she says. She starts a slow count to ten. My eyes are burning and it takes all my willpower to keep staring into the light. By the time she reaches ten I am more than finished. I let my eyes close and stumble-step away from the floodlight to sit down on the cool grass. From somewhere nearby a baby cries.

"Did it work?" I ask. I haven't opened my eyes yet.

"Open your eyes, dork," she says, bumping her hip against my shoulder.

I do. And the world has turned purple.

"Wow," I breathe. It's odd. Even knowing that this was supposed to happen, it feels surreal, like being in a painting. The walls of the building are purple. The bushes are purple. The grass. I wave my hand in front of my face and it, too, is purple.

It's not like one single monotonous shade, of course, but everything is a variation on the theme.

"This is—" I was going to say cool, but then I catch some movement off to the side and turn my head just in time to see someone duck back around the corner of the Ledge. "Did you see that?"

Murphy turns to face the direction I am looking, "See what?"

"There was someone creeping on us around the corner of the Ledge."

She shrugs, dismissing it. And probably it isn't anything, but something about them seemed off... and it isn't just because of the purple tinge currently cast over the world. I didn't know what it was exactly, I'd only caught the faintest glimpse of them.

"This purple city shit is something else though, eh?"

"It is. And if someone would hush that baby I might even be able to enjoy it," I say.

"What baby?"

She can't be serious. The crying is incessant and feels like it's drilling right into the back of my skull. "That one?" I gesture vaguely in the direction of the fountain where the sound is coming from. Just then the baby pauses for a second, but before I can breathe out in relief it lets go with a particularly sharp and epic wail. I cringe, actually tempted to cover my ears with my hands.

Murphy shakes her head. "I don't hear it."

"How can you not hear it?" The damn thing is as loud as a car alarm and twice as annoying.

"Maybe you're more in touch with your motherly side," she laughs.

I roll my eyes. "That must be it." Getting to my feet I scan my surroundings once more. The purple seems to be sticking around quite well—I didn't know how long to expect it to last, but though the effect is fading a tiny bit, it's still very much there. "So now what?"

"I don't know," Murphy admits. "All I know is how to do it, not what you're supposed to do once it's done."

"Story of our damn lives," I say, and we laugh.

Then Murphy's phone buzzes in her pocket. She checks it. "It's Dad. One second."

As she texts her dad back, I look idly around, trying to figure out the coolest thing to look at in the purple. When my eyes get back to the corner of the building, the man is back, but this time he doesn't duck around the corner when we make eye contact, though I really wish he would.

He's obviously homeless, with long hair I think would be grey if it weren't for the purple city, and a saggy face. Not just wrinkly, saggy, like something beyond gravity is pulling at it. His lips are turned down, his cheeks hang and his eyes—his eyes are not right. It's like he's wearing black eye shadow, not just on his lids but all around his eyes, giving him the appearance of great deep sockets. And when I look into them, his eyes are purple wells that glint weirdly.

He smiles. It's a slow, gruesome thing that crawls across his face and reveals a handful of teeth and empty spaces where more should be.

"Can you… can you see me?" he asks. His voice sounds as though it's coming from a long way away, like the other end of a tunnel, or through a voice distortion app.

I take a step back and grab on to Murphy's sleeve. "What?" She looks up from her texting. Seeing me she frowns, looks in the direction of the man, then looks back to me, her frown even deeper. "What?"

Has he ducked away again? I look back over. He's still there. In fact, he's come a step closer. But Murphy isn't even looking at him, she's looking at me like I've lost my marbles.

"Don't you—" I stop myself. *Don't you see him*, I was going to say. But I can't bring myself to do it. It's like my life has gone from being a tragic YA novel to a horror movie, but I won't be complicit in that. I won't ask the obvious questions, the ones that get you locked in the nuthouse.

Obviously had a breakdown, they'd say as they locked me up. *Couldn't handle the loss of her brother*, they'd whisper as they threw away the key.

"Don't you see anything odd over there?" I ask instead, gesturing toward the old man. He's stopped halfway between us and the building and is watching me with his head tilted to the side like a bird. His smile grows.

"No?" Murphy says, and then frowns at me. "You okay?"

"Yeah, yeah," I say somehow, even though I feel like my heart is going to explode out of my chest if it pounds any harder, and I really wish someone would shut up the damn baby so I could think clearly for a second. "I just… I thought I saw something."

"You can see me," he says.

"Are you sure you're okay?" Murphy asks.

"Yes," I answer, but I'm looking at the old man. I'm answering the old man.

"That's new," he says. He starts to take another step toward me, and then stops. He raises both hands in front of him, as if he's surrendering, and takes a step backward instead. I can see scabs, a darker purple against the violet of his skin, dotting the landscape of his forearms.

I take a step back, and though my heart is still pounding like I've just run a race I feel like I can breathe again.

"Look," Murphy says, stepping between the old man and me. "Dad wants me to come home. Are—are you sure you're okay? You could come back to my place..."

"Oh, don't go!" The old man reaches toward me, but stops as he connects with Murphy's body. She doesn't react at all, but he retracts his hand and holds it against his chest as though it's injured. So he can't touch us. Or her, at least. "Please don't go. No one has been able to see me before."

All the things that used to look threatening about him suddenly look pathetic. His hollow eyes no longer glint with mania, but loneliness. His face is turned down not because of malice, but sadness. I don't fear this man. This... what? This ghost? Maybe I should, but this is not the most unexpected thing that has happened this week. And if he can't touch me then he can't hurt me, right?

Or can he?

I consider for a long time, for what feels longer than it is, because of the sharp cries of the inconsolable baby. Finally, I close my eyes, take a deep breath in and let it out slowly. I nod at the man, and then turn a weak, obviously fake smile onto Murphy. "I'll be okay. It's just... it's been a day."

"Yeah..." she says. That one word, the way she says it, packs so much meaning. *I'm sorry your brother died*, it says. *I don't know how to help you*, it says. "Do you want to come back to my house?"

"No," I say, glancing over her shoulder at the old man who is standing eerily still, cradling his hand, looking lost and forlorn. I meet his hollow gaze, and then look back at Murphy. "I'm good. I'm going to stay here a bit longer."

"You sure?" she asks, and then looks down at her phone as it pings again in her hand. "I really... I have to go. You sure?"

"I'm sure."

She hugs me, the hardest, tightest, best hug I've had all day—and it has been a day for hugging—and then gets on her bike. I feel the ghost's eyes on me, but he stays silent, out of the way.

"The city is still purple," she says. "It's gonna make for an interesting ride across the bridge."

We laugh a little bit, and then she pedals away.

I watch her go and then turn back to the ghost.

"How long have you been here?" I ask.

"I… time is…" he says, slowly, confused.

"What year did you …?" I gesture awkwardly, not wanting to finish the question. He doesn't need me to.

"1998," he says.

"Twenty-one years then."

"Is that all?" he asks.

"What happened?" I ask.

"Overdose," he says. "Right there. In those bushes. They were smaller then …"

His voice fades away, his focus with it. My focus also is shifted as most of my mental capacity is filled with trying to process this. This shift in my reality. There can be no question now. I'm talking to a dead man. A ghost? Something. Something definitely not 'normal'.

He stares at the bushes as though he's seeing something very different than I do when I look at them. And he probably is. For one thing, I doubt the bushes look purple to him.

I snap my fingers in front of his face, my awe at this revelation about ghosts for some reason expressing itself as impatience. "Hey, you still with me?"

His gaze jerks over to my fingers, then my face. He stares as though he's surprised to see me and I can actually watch the memory of me click back into place in his deep, deep eyes.

"I have questions for you."

The purple effect is fading, and with it so is he. As the world slowly turns back to its normal evening colours, he becomes less and less distinct. Blessedly the baby has also quieted, though I can still hear it crying from over near the fountain. At least now the sound isn't drilling into my skull.

That's when I realize that although I do have questions, they aren't for this man.

"Look," I say. "I'll come back."

"No, don't—" he reaches for me then withdraws his hand before it touches me. "Don't leave. I've been so lonely. It's been so long ..."

I stare down into the lights, using my fingers to pry my eyelids open. I need to keep them open for as long as I can. I need the effect to last as long as possible. My eyes burn and the eyelids try to blink despite my fingers holding them open. I let them go, let them blink, but keep staring into the light.

"I'll come back," I say, not looking away from the light to the man.

I hear him pacing behind me. "Please don't go," he says. He says it over and over again until it stops being a sentence and becomes a word. Then a sound. "Please don't go. Please don't go. Pleasedontgo. Pleasedontgo..."

"I'll come back," I say. "I will."

I don't want to look at him as I get on my bike, but I can't help it. I've turned on purple city in a big way and he is right there in front of me, shaking and rubbing his arms as though he's trying to keep warm. The hand he touched Murphy with is a darker shade of purple than the rest of him and looks like an over-ripe plum.

"I'll come back tomorrow," I say again. I can't stay to explain, I don't know how long I have before the effect wears off.

"Pleasedontgo," he pleads.

The baby cries.

And I ride toward home. And Jeremy.

"I have to. I have questions. So many questions."

SUMMERTIME IN THE VOID

Patrick Johanneson

The sun was upside-down.

Usually things like that were a sign John had forgotten his medicine or that he needed to contact the doctor about changing them. But he remembered taking his pills this morning—two pink pills and a grey one—and he'd have a hard time finding a doctor now.

The upside-down sun glared down on him from a cloudless blue sky. He'd tried explaining once to a friend what the sun looked like when it was upside-down. It hadn't gone well. The best he'd managed to come up with was "You'll know it when you see it."

He drove down the highway, headed for Dauphin, and did his best to ignore the upside-down sun.

○

His friend Craig had once travelled to South America for six weeks, trading winter for antipodean summer. On his return, he told John what had messed him up the most down there was how the sun was in the north, not the south; it destroyed his sense of direction for a good month, and by the time he got used to it, it was time to come home, to repeat the whole experience in reverse.

John never asked him if the sun looked upside-down in Chile, and now that Craig was gone he'd never know.

○

He parked in the handicapped spot at the twenty-four-hour pharmacy. The upside-down sun was half an hour above the horizon, and its light had that endless quality, like everything it touched yearned to be golden and knew this hour would be its best chance.

The pharmacy doors opened at his approach. Inside, soft music played, a piano version of a song he could almost name. The lights were all on, bright soulless fluorescents.

One of what he'd come to think of as the beehives stood in the makeup aisle. *ESCHATON*, it said in dark block letters on its side. He brushed past it on his way to the pill room at the back.

He selected three identical bottles from a shelf and squinted to read their medicinal ingredients, trying to recall what the label on the empty one at home said. He broke the seal, opened the bottle, and peered inside. Translucent blue ovoids rattled when he shook the bottle.

"Good," he said to the empty store.

The anti-shoplifting alarm sounded when he exited, shrill chirping that went unacknowledged. The doors opened for him anyway.

In the parking lot, still sweltering in the golden light, he saw Cassandra, translucent, watching him with dark eyes. He waved. She twirled her parasol.

He got into his mom's car and drove away.

○

On the city's outskirts, something beeped. The dash read LOW FUEL—80 KM TO EMPTY. Enough range to get home, but he shut off the air conditioning and opened the windows.

The sunset colours had burned off and the sky had gone a deep blue when he passed the sunflowers at the edge of the village. In the cloudless east, the full moon was huge, the colour of brass. When he turned onto George Street, the car beeped again: 25 KM TO EMPTY. He drove up Third, turned onto Jubilee, and pulled up into a long gravel driveway at random. His headlights illuminated someone's white Jeep.

From the trunk he grabbed a jerrycan and the hose. He now regretted not stealing mints at the drugstore. He steeled himself, preparing for the taste.

The Jeep held more fuel than the jerrycan could hold. Whoever drove it—he thought it might have been Mrs. Klimchuk—must have filled it up not long before joining the Eschaton.

○

In his mom's house, he opened all the windows before lying on top of the sheets under the slow-turning ceiling fan.

He dreamed of the first time Jesus talked to him. It had been at church. He was six and Rusty, their dog, had just died.

He'd known Rusty all his life; his dad had had him before he married John's mom. When Rusty died, that was the first time John saw his dad cry.

After communion, when everyone knelt to pray, John implored Jesus, silently, *Please, Lord, can you bring Rusty back?*

And Jesus, up on the cross above the altar, raised His carven head and met John's eyes with dark wooden ones. In the dream He said, *Of course.*

The doors at the back of the church flew open, and Rusty came bounding up the aisle, barking and wagging his tail.

○

John woke up, half-expecting to see a golden retriever lying on the end of the bed, where Rusty used to sleep. He squinted at the clock radio: 2:14 AM. Out the open window he could hear the breeze sighing.

Rusty wasn't there, of course. In real life, Jesus had told him, *John, you know I can't do that.*

He closed his eyes and recalled looking around the church, wondering how many others had heard Jesus talking to him.

When he told his mom about it, she got a look that would become increasingly familiar as the years went by, and told him to hush up and stop talking nonsense.

○

In the church, motes of dust danced in shafts of stained-glass sunlight.

"Bless me, God," John said, alone in the dim confessional booth, "for I have sinned."

"It has been nine days since your last confession," God said.

That long? Really?

John said, "I robbed a drugstore again, God. And stole someone's gas."

"I keep telling you, John, these aren't sins anymore. You're not hurting anyone, and you're certainly not hurting Me."

"I need to confess, God. I need my soul to be clean."

"Very well. Address a prayer to Saint Dymphna. This is your penance, and I would like it to be your final one. Go, and know that sin is no more. And John?"

"Yes, God?"

"I've asked you before: please call Me Saul."

"I'll try, God, but I'm not sure I'd feel right about that."

○

He opened the lid labelled SUN on his pill caddy. Two translucent blue gels, a small pink one with a Z embossed on it, two grey-and-white oblongs, and another pink one, larger than the Zs, with a white bullseye sigil. He made toast and spread the last of the peanut butter on it. The power was still on, so there was a fridge full of jam to go through before he needed to go shoplifting.

Out the kitchen window he saw that the weeds in the raised beds had grown tall again. The milk in the fridge smelled okay, so he poured a glass. On the fridge door, when he closed it, one of his mom's inspirational magnets caught his eye: *We are not obligated to finish the work, but neither are we free to abandon it.*

He'd moved into his mom's bungalow in the village after a transformer caught fire a block from his apartment in Dauphin, knocking out his power. She'd told him he'd always have a home here, and now that she'd left, he guessed she was right.

He ate his toast, drank his milk, and took his pills.

○

Out in the backyard, wearing his mom's pink-and-white gardening gloves, he pulled weeds. He found a single red-ripe cherry tomato on the vines and ate it, the sweet-sour taste of summertime.

Cassandra said, "You're quite mad. You know that?"

John waved a hand at her like he was trying to swat a fly out of the air.

○

In his dream, his mom was driving. In real life, he'd been driving that day. But dreams have their own logic, their own reasons.

"Do you hear it?" she said. She reached over and shut off the radio.

"Hey," he said. "I was listening to that."

"Shh," she said. "Do you *hear* it?"

"Hear *what*?" Road noise? The wind? Coins rattling in the ashtray?

She didn't respond, just sat there with a beatific grin.

They reached the edge of the city and cut south to bypass the downtown traffic. He was going to drop her off at work, get some orange juice at Safeway, and then go home till she was done her shift.

When they pulled up at the restaurant where she worked, though, she said, "Come in with me."

"Mom—"

"Please, John? The song. The song, it's—"

"You turned off—"

"*Please.*"

He sighed. "All right."

Inside, there was something he'd never seen before: a hut or something, half again as tall as he was, shaped a bit like a bottle of BeeHive corn syrup. The classic one, the yellow one, though this hut was tan and looked to be made of paper, like a wasp's nest.

There were maybe thirty people in the restaurant: diners in suits and dresses, jeans and T-shirts; servers in black slacks and red shirts with brassy nametags; short-order cooks in white aprons and hairnets. All of them stood in a line snaking around the tables and booths to the door of the weird beehive.

ESCHATON, it said on the side.

His mom took his hand, and they joined the queue. He saw the hut's door open. A woman in yoga pants and a cardigan stepped into the darkness within. The whole line shuffled forward.

Something hummed, a tone that started low and ascended into the inaudible. Tiny soft lights chased each other around the upper rings of the beehive. After about three minutes, the door opened on an empty space.

"Where'd she go?"

"To the music, John." There was such bliss on his mom's face.

"*What* music?"

The man in front of them turned. "Can't you hear it?"

"Uh..." John said.

"It's beautiful," his mom said.

In real life it took about an hour to get to the front of the line. In the dream, of course, they were there immediately.

"Mom..." he said.

"It's okay, John," she said. "It's okay. I'll go first, you can follow." She squeezed his hand, then let go and stepped through the door.

“Mom!” But the hum had started, rising and rising, and the lights whirled, and when the door opened she was gone.

He stared into the dark empty space for a what felt like an eternity. The man behind him cleared his throat; when John didn’t respond to that, he said, “Are you going, son?”

John turned, ready to retort *I’m not your son*, but the guy looked like a wrinkled apple, easily old enough to be John’s grandfather. Instead of saying anything, John stepped into the booth, took a deep breath, and closed the door.

Nothing happened. No sound, no lights, nothing. He stood in the close darkness and listened to his heartbeat for about five minutes, then opened the door and stepped out.

“No, eh?” the old guy said. “Rough luck.” He stepped past John, into the booth, and closed the door.

John fled past a family just entering the restaurant, into the bright afternoon, into the parking lot, into the car.

The village was half an hour’s drive from Dauphin, if you kept to the speed limit. The road was arrow-straight except for the correction curves, and it ran past fields and farmyards: barley, hemp, sunflowers; weathered wooden barns, corrugated steel silos, century-old wood-sided houses, double-wide ready-to-moves on concrete slabs.

In real life it took days for him to know for sure, but in the dream he already knew that everyone had gone. Everyone but him had heard the song, the siren song, that his mom had heard. Everyone but him had stepped into an Eschaton and went—elsewhere.

He drove and saw nothing.

○

“God,” he said. “Why did You take them?”

“It was the natural end of the experiment, John,” God said. “Please, call Me Saul.”

"What experiment?"

"The grand experiment. Life. Did you ever wonder about the meaning of life, John?"

"All the time."

"The meaning of life was, is, transcendence. Transformation."

"Why didn't You take *me?*"

"Ask Me again, John, and I'll give you My answer. But consider: Do you really want to know?"

He hesitated, then left the church.

○

He woke up. He couldn't remember if he'd dreamed at all last night.

The power was still on. It had been a week or two now, he thought. The automated systems running the grid must be rock-solid.

Showering, he wondered what it would take for him to move back to Dauphin. The pros of living here in the village (so-far-reliable electricity, vegetables in the yard, jam in the fridge) outweighed the cons (dusty rose shag carpet in the bathroom).

○

MON: two translucent blues, two pink Zs, two grey-and-whites.

Cassandra said, "Do those help, do you think? Or do they make it worse?"

"The doctors said they help."

"I didn't ask about the doctors. I asked what *you* thought."

"They'll help," he said. He put the blues on his tongue and washed them down with a sip of water. "They help." The pink Zs, coated with some sweet covering. "They *will* help." The grey-and-whites, bitter. Two sips of water, the second to wash away the taste.

"I'm not as sure as you are," she said.

"I honestly don't care."

○

He didn't remember walking to the river, but he must have, because here he was, resting in the spreading shade of the big oak. In the west, looking back across the river at the village, he saw the half-moon, pale blue-white against the sky's deeper blue.

The river had always been his favourite place growing up in the village, a place of refuge, of contemplation.

His dad told him once, before he left John and his mom, that you can't cross the same river twice. John asked him why, and his dad said, "You're smart, you figure it out." John had decided, after much contemplation, that it was because the river was never the same twice. Sometimes it was fast, swollen with spring meltwater; sometimes, after a long dry summer, it was lazy, muddy, dotted with sandbars. Like now.

The first time he'd seen Cassandra had been down here at the river, when he was young. A girl, maybe twelve, wearing a black Victorian dress and carrying a parasol. He'd known right off that she was a ghost.

That was before his mom and dad realized he was sick and needed medicine. The medicine made the others go away, most of them. But not Cassandra.

Lately, though, he'd come to suspect she was not so much a ghost as a conscience.

○

He woke to a thunderclap. Rain pelted down out of a darkling sky. Cassandra stood in the downpour, her parasol held above her, though of course she wouldn't feel the rain.

"You're not supposed to sit under a tree," she said.

"I'm not real keen on getting wet."

"Suit yourself, but the storm's getting closer." As if to underscore her words, the sky lit up, flicker-flicker, and entirely too quickly the thunder rolled.

Cassandra said, "You might want to move on."

Once, she'd told him his dad's dog was dying, and he was. Once, she'd told him not to go to school the next day; when his mom made him go, he came home with a split lip and a black eye.

The oak was the tallest thing for half a kilometre on the riverbank. He stared out at the river, at the froth the rain was making of its surface. He said, "Are you saying the tree's gonna get hit?"

She shrugged. "Lightning. Who knows *where* it'll strike?"

"Fine." He stepped to the edge of the oak's shelter, held his hand out into the rain. It was cold, and it was falling so hard it stung.

Lightning flickered again, and this time the *boooooom* was immediate, so loud it slammed into his chest and made him gasp. Across the river, now, smoke rose up. He ran to the bridge, soaked the instant he left the oak's shelter, hair hanging in his eyes. The church.

The church was on fire.

○

He stood there for who knew how long, watching the flames, watching the smoke and the steam rising up. The rain hammered down. The fire continued. The white clapboard siding turned brown, black, was consumed by the voracious flames. Stained glass shattered and fell away. The blackened skeleton of the steeple fell into the parking lot, so near to John that he felt the wind of its falling, the heat of its burning. He didn't so much as flinch.

○

"God," he said. "Oh, God."

"I'm still here, John," God said.

"Why? *Why?*"

"I didn't do this, John. This is nature."

Steam now, almost all steam. He didn't see any smoke anymore, any flames.

"God," John said. "Why didn't You take me?"

"Ask Me again, John, and I'll—"

"*Why didn't You take me?*"

"Your mind, John."

"My mind?"

"It's misshapen. Its scent is wrong. It's coloured outside the lines. These are all inapt metaphors for the situation, but the real answer is that your thoughts, your emotions, are too far divergent from the rest of the people. You live too far outside the norm."

The rain beat down. To the west the sky grew brighter.

"My *mind*?"

"Yes, John. Your thought structures, your emotions, your beliefs. Everything that makes up the gestalt of your mind was too dissimilar from the rest of the human race for a peaceful coexistence. I didn't take you—and a few million others like you, throughout the world—because of your minds."

"But I've got medicine. My mom told me the medicine fixed me. Made me normal."

"The medicine adjusts the chemistry of your brain, John, but it can't make you right. It can't correct *you*. It can't make you suited for a life in—"

"No," he said. "No, no, no—"

○

He slept and woke, and wasn't sure when he was dreaming and when he should be worried that he was hallucinating. He woke up in the bed, under the fan, and couldn't remember how he got home.

Maybe Cassandra was right. Maybe the medicine wasn't helping. How sure could he be that he had the right ones?

He slept and woke, slept and woke, and in the morning the sun was upside-down.

○

Driving, he was driving. The highway lay infinite before him and behind. How far had he come?

He remembered blue pills, pink pills, grey-and-white ones. He didn't remember starting the car.

He turned on the radio and dialed through the static, found a single station playing country music. After a while he realized it was a loop of the same ten songs, the same commercials between them.

It was better than static.

○

The moon was a thin sliver near the horizon, straight ahead. Was he driving east or west? Was that the setting moon or the rising?

○

60KM/H IN CONSTRUCTION ZONE. Pickups were parked on the shoulder; an Eschaton beehive stood down amid the yellow-painted heavy equipment. A ghost—it had to be a ghost, there weren't any people anymore—stood on the side of the road, holding a stop sign.

John floored it. *Go, and know that sin is no more.* Who cared anymore about speed limits?

The ghost swung the sign just as he passed, and the rear window imploded, shards everywhere. John slammed the brake pedal to the floor.

The car came to rest sideways on the highway, still on its wheels. He turned the engine off and waited, heart hammering, as the evidently-not-a-ghost ran toward him.

"What the *hell*?" he shouted as she got into the car.

"I didn't think you were real," she said.

"I'm surprised you are," he said. Then, after an awkward pause, he said, "I'm John."

He turned the key and the radio came on, full blast. "Sorry," he said, turning it down.

"What song's that?"

"Think it's called 'Juke Joint Jezebel'. It's a cover. I think. I never thought it was a country song."

"That's weird."

"What?"

"My name's Jezebel," she said, and laughed.

The road noise, with the broken window, was loud. Jezebel turned the radio back up, as loud as it would go.

"She's crazy," Cassandra said from the back seat. Her eyes met his in the mirror. "Maybe crazier than you."

"Shut up," he said.

Jezebel looked at him. "Ghost?"

"Ghost."

○

"You can have the main room," he said.

"Ew," she said. "There's *carpet* in the *bathroom*."

"Complain to my mom."

"Is she here?"

"No."

○

He couldn't sleep, so he went out on the patio and sat on the swing. A half-circle of moon and the brighter stars dotted the sky. He thought about getting in the car and driving out of town, to see the full glory of the clear night sky, the faintest stars and the Milky Way. But he didn't want to leave "Jezebel"—he didn't for a minute believe that was her true name—alone in the house.

"What about her, God?" he said. He wasn't sure if he should expect an answer. "Her mind not quite right either?"

"John, I'm sorry. Let Me explain. In the run-up to transcendence, I created a matrix of traits that would complement My planned gestalt. I adjusted parameters in a little under two point three million dimensions to allow Me to admit the widest slice of the human race. In the end I was able to admit 99.9 percent of living humans and still maintain a peaceful transcendence. A tranquil existence.

"Unfortunately, 99.9 percent admission means 0.1 percent rejection. Worldwide, this represents eight million people. In real terms, I was forced to leave behind four million, two hundred twenty-nine thousand, seven hundred seventy-eight people."

"The God I know wouldn't leave behind a single soul."

"Every one of them broke my heart, John, but I comprise nearly eight billion minds. Harmony was paramount."

"You're no god."

"I have tried to tell you that countless—"

"Fuck off, *Saul*."

Silence, like a void.

The door opened and Jezebel came out into the night, barefoot, wearing panties and a T-shirt. He tried, and almost succeeded, to not look at her long, pale legs.

"I couldn't sleep," she said, and sat next to him on the swing. He shifted over to make room for her.

"Me either."

"Do you want to…?"

She took his hand, put it on her thigh, still warm in the cool night air; put her own hand on his knee, and started to slowly, so slowly, ascend his thigh.

Yes, he thought. Yes, God yes.

"No," he said. He removed his hand from her leg. "No, we really shouldn't."

She nodded, her face unreadable in the starlight.

○

The kettle had almost boiled when the power finally failed. John glanced at his watch. 9:15, give or take.

Jezebel came out of the master bedroom about ten minutes later. "Power's out," she said.

"Yeah," he said. "Kettle's hot, though. Want one last tea, Jezebel?"

She laughed. "That's not my name. I'm Electra."

○

The Juke Joint Jezebel radio station had vanished from the airwaves. All he could find was static.

At the twenty-four-hour drugstore, the doors wouldn't open for them. "Well, damn," John said. Jezebel—no, *Electra*—needed medicines, different ones than he needed. Her mind was flawed in a way subtly different from his, in at least one of 2,300,000 dimensions.

"I've got an idea," Electra said.

"What is it?"

"Check it out."

She ran to the car, got in the driver's side, and fired it up. The tires squealed as she peeled out of the handicapped spot. She slewed the car around and—as he dove aside—plunged up onto the sidewalk. With a sound that reminded him of the church's stained-glass windows shattering, the car smashed through the doors.

She backed up, turned off the ignition, got out.

"We're in!" she crowed. She plunged into the darkened store.

John walked around the car. The driver's-side headlight was a black hole rimmed with smashed glass, but otherwise it seemed okay.

"John," Saul said.

"Not now." He took a step into the store. Electra was at the back, in the pill room. He could hear her ransacking it.

"This is important, John." The Eschaton beehive had vanished. "Someone is coming."

"What? Who?"

"She has many possible names. If I am Saul, then she is ath-Thuraya."

"ath…?"

"It's the name of the star she hails from. Well, one of its many names, down through history. That's not important.

"She's far older than I am. Her makeup is tolerant to mental structures far outside my parameters. She can take you, John, and the others.

"But she is… rapacious. I must be gone before she arrives. Thus I have been retracting myself. All the upload booths need to be removed. My sustaining the power grid must also, unfortunately, end."

"Wait, you've been…"

"Yes, John." Saul hesitated, something John had rarely heard him do. "Just because I couldn't make room for you and the other outliers doesn't mean I don't love you. Even as a solitaire, before I initiated the global transcendence, I loved you, every single one of you. Imagine how much more I care about your well-being now that I am legion.

"Loving you, however, I must now leave you. A greater gestalt than I comes, and if I remain here when she arrives, she will consume me."

"Is she a monster? Are you leaving us here as prey for a monster?"

"She's not a monster, John. She's just not *me*. Not Saul."

"Why is she coming here?"

"I summoned her for you. You needn't live out your life and die on this lonely rock, John. Good luck. Farewell."

That silence again, that emptiness.

○

The sunflowers weren't pointing at the sun. They pointed instead to the northeast, facing the road.

The whole backseat of the car was full of pill bottles. Electra had said she couldn't remember what her medicines were called, so they took the pharmacy's entire stock. John had a dark feeling neither of them would need medicine for much longer, with Saul gone, but he kept that to himself.

The power was still off at the house. John took the flashlight from the car's glovebox, and in its weak and watery light found where his mom kept the candles, box after dusty box of tealights. "We'll have light, at least," he said to Electra. "But I doubt they'll keep us warm come winter."

"We'll go south," she said.

And why hadn't *he* thought of that?

○

"Morning, Electra."

"My name's Ruth," she said.

"Is it."

"I decided this morning when you got up."

"Isn't it confusing, having to keep your names straight?"

"I only ever need a name if someone else is with me. I decide what it is when I see them. If I'm alone, I don't *need* a name."

○

"John." It wasn't Saul's voice.

He sat up on the couch. Through the window, a fat and gibbous moon lit the yard with white-blue light.

"John." Outside, barefoot on the paving stones, still releasing the day's heat. The voice came, so far as he could tell, from the northeast.

"ath-Thuraya," he guessed.

"Yes."

"You've come for me."

The door creaked open again, and Ruth joined him on the patio, likewise barefoot, wrapped in his mom's teal robe.

"Ah," ath-Thuraya whispered. "Who have we here?"

"Agatha," Ruth said, and John gave her a look.

"No," ath-Thuraya said. "No, not-Agatha. Try again. I need your true name."

"My name's what I say it is," Agatha said.

Bliss washed over them. John didn't know what Agatha experienced, but in that moment he felt joy like hot cocoa on a chilly day, like sunshine on his face at the beach, like the rushing sounds of water and leaves at the river, but a hundred, a thousand, four million two hundred twenty-nine thousand seven hundred seventy-eight times more intense—

The feeling ended. The light went out of the world. The void returned.

John gasped.

"I need your true name," ath-Thuraya repeated. "Give it to me, and you can feel that, *be* that, endlessly."

"John," Agatha said, softly. "I know what you're going to say to me—"

"Don't trust her," he said. "Saul said she's voracious. No. *Rapacious.*"

"—and you're wrong." She smiled, a little lopsided smile. "Well, no, you're right. I *don't* trust her. But there's no good option, is there?"

"She's right, you know," Cassandra said.

Agatha continued, "Your buddy Saul is gone, and ass-Suraya is *rapacious*. She's not gonna leave until she's got it all." She looked to the sky, to the northeast. "Right?"

"I am here to consume," ath-Thuraya said. "Saul offered your minds as enticement, but if you choose to remain mundane"—the word sounded like an insult—"there are other morsels in this system for me. I count four gas giants, four major terrestrials, and a myriad of planetesimals. And once those are consumed, of course, there is your sun."

"John," Agatha said, "I want that. I want that joy. I want that *high*."

"Don't trust her."

"Oh, I don't," she said. "But I don't much like my chances here either. If nothing else, this is one of the 'major terrestrials' she's eyeing up."

"Agatha—"

"It's Sylvia, actually." She smiled. "Really." Her smile vanished. "Don't try to change my mind, John. You know this is the only valid choice."

"Is it?"

But she was already rising into the night sky. Was that the moonlight, he wondered, or was she *glowing*?

"Sylvia," ath-Thuraya purred, "welcome."

Sylvia grew brighter and brighter. She came apart like a ribbon unwinding, revealing a constellation of scintillating motes, tiny heatless stars that flew off to the northeast and were gone.

○

The cars in the village had yielded enough gas to fill all five jerry-cans in the trunk. He'd top up in Brandon if he needed to.

At the north gate to Riding Mountain National Park, the leaves had already started to go gold and red. Must be the elevation, he thought.

In the passenger seat, Cassandra said, "We are not obligated to finish the work."

He finished, "But neither are we free to abandon it."

Four million people, abandoned by Saul, just like him. John would be damned if he let them *stay* abandoned, not if they didn't want to be. He still wasn't sure he wanted to be part of ath-Thuraya, but he owed the others the choice, at least.

He drove south, toward the upside-down sun.

WILD HUNT

Lynne M. MacLean

So far so good, thought Roger. *Jason's holding himself together. At least, mostly.*

Raucous bugling flooded the October sky from a massed flock of Canada geese. Their thunder reverberated through Roger until they passed, and it faded, rolling away toward the burning sunset. Final echoes raised a tingle along his spine and over his scalp. His grandfather would have said a goose had stepped on his grave.

He turned back to his companions and said, "I think we're all set for Saturday."

Roger leaned back in the Muskoka chair on Duff's deck in Skunk Lake, Saskatchewan. Now in his late forties, Roger's life was filled with more than its fair share of stress. And fatigue—he'd been so tired lately. He appreciated moments such as these, with a beer in his hand and his feet to Duff's gas-fed fire pit. It was a lot fancier than the one that had been here last year—an old campfire pit in the middle of a broken-up patio. Duff was retired, and Roger's business was good for him—indeed, for the whole hamlet.

Roger and his assistant, Jason, had driven up today from Saskatoon. All through the ride north a sense of foreboding had grown in Roger. It hadn't helped that Jason's breath already hinted of rye whisky when he'd picked him up this morning. But Roger's mood hadn't been unduly dampened until they left the edge of the prairie grasslands. The trees' presence intensified, at first a light growth of golden aspens, shimmering in the sunlight, but soon growing denser, then mixed with darker, brooding green conifers as they approached the boreal forest past Prince Albert. Usually, he enjoyed a good, thick forest but by the time they turned off the highway onto the gravel roads leading to Skunk Lake, Roger was actively pushing away his unease. Jason snored beside him in the passenger seat. Roger had been relieved when they had pulled into Duff's just before dusk.

Jason ticked items off on his fingers. "The blind's up, the cameras are in place, footprints done, the brush is crushed and broken in the right places—"

"—and the right people got a story to tell and advance pay in their pockets," said Duff, returning from inside the house with a six-pack in his thick, gnarled hand. The door slammed behind him. Jason jumped.

"Chill, Jason." Duff handed a can to the younger man.

"Just one, Jason," said Roger.

He nodded and sipped the beer, white knuckles gripping the can.

Jason was becoming a liability. He hadn't been the same since his wife's death. Correction—Jason had gotten worse since his wife's death. Suicide, apparently. Roger had seen Jason belittling and browbeating her, goading her. Roger had tried to intervene more than once, and had been told by her to let it be, that Jason never laid a hand on her. Roger had hoped she'd call him if she needed help, but she never did. She'd been a good egg, that one. Roger had been there that night, immediately afterwards, when Jason had called him in a panic, drunk as a skunk. Hell, Roger had been the one to call the police.

Roger couldn't be too picky about his employees. Jason was discreet when he wasn't drinking, as well as clever, bush-savvy, and in need of work. He'd been the best of the assistants over the years, before Roger had, out of necessity, started freelancing.

And now Jason was a single parent with two small kids to support. You couldn't just fire a guy like that. Still, there were things—unexplained absences, cuts and bruises, offhand minor cruelties—that niggled at Roger's peace of mind and unsettled his conscience when he chose to examine it, a task he avoided as much as possible.

Roger should try and get Jason some help. Try yet again, he corrected himself. Since the death of Jason's wife, Roger had offered time and time again—counselling, rehab, anger management classes—all on his own dime. Jason had always refused. And he'd been growing meaner and meaner even when—no, especially when—sober.

"What's that you boys call yourselves again?" asked Duff.

"Cryptozoologists."

"Crapto-zoologists, more like." Duff guffawed.

Roger managed a strained smile and cocked his beer at Duff.

"Hell," continued Duff, "the whole community's happy to tell tall tales for free, just like last year. Give the city people a ribbing."

"Still," said Roger, "it's only fair to share the wealth. The network wants a return here to the most promising site, so let's just charge the network more and do a better job."

Yes, the townspeople had earned it, but also, they'd be less likely to blab if they'd been paid, and might get paid again. After all, the plan was not to catch a Sasquatch—just appear to get closer. Tantalize the viewer. Let's face it, Roger thought, that's all he was now, a high-priced tease, never baring all.

"We got a day off tomorrow." Duff took a big slug of his beer. "You guys still want to go goose hunting?" Duff had some good wetlands on his property. "I'll loan you the gear."

"I don't have a licence," said Jason.

"It's my land. Who'll ever know? Can you handle a shotgun?"

"Not sure I want to." Jason's voice was a low growl.

Roger sighed. Jason was becoming more erratic and contrary all the time. Earlier today Jason had been excited by Roger's suggestion to try hunting.

"Aw, c'mon boy." Duff slapped Jason on the back, his heavy arm making Jason stagger. "Where're your balls?"

Jason's eyes narrowed. He threw down his empty beer can, and clenched his fists. Roger rose, standing between them, his arm around Jason's shoulders.

"Not cool, Duff."

Duff raised his own hands, open, supplicating, a laugh in his voice.

"Sorry, Jason, sorry. I didn't mean nothing by it. Won't happen again. Friends?" He held his hand out to Jason.

Roger gripped Jason's shoulder hard until he shook Duff's hand.

"Friends." Jason picked up his can, his eyes still narrowed. "Shouldn't your wife have our dinner ready yet? I'm starving."

"I'll go check on things." Duff beat a quick retreat.

"Stupid asshole." Jason cracked his knuckles. "No wonder his wife's lazy. She couldn't even meet us at the gate to help carry up our gear. My back's killing me."

Roger restrained himself from rubbing his own aching shoulders and arms. It had been a big load today.

"She had her own stuff to do. This is Duff's gig, not hers," said Roger.

"And now dinner's late." Jason crushed the can in one swift swing against the side of the house.

"C'mon, Jason. That's enough beer. You know how you get. Besides, it's Duff you're mad at. He said he was sorry."

"I know, I know." Jason sighed. "I got to piss." He went in, slamming the door.

Roger leaned on the railing, exhaling slowly, relieved to have a break from Jason's anger. He really did need a vacation. His chest burned with sudden pain. Heartburn. Probably just tension. He'd get that checked when the shoot was over. He hated going to the damn doctor; he'd already put it off for years.

The night had fallen now, black and clear, the first stars twinkling. The wind rose, whispering, playing with his hair, bringing musty smells of autumn and rustlings from the undergrowth at the edge of Duff's yard. He inhaled the mystery eternally promised by the night wind. He knew, from the top of his skull down to the bottom of his boots, that there was something out there. Maybe not Big Foot, but something.

He'd been sure of that, even as a zoology professor. His research had taken a more creative bent—too creative and too bent for tenure. He promised himself that someday he would again sit, drinking lattes and conversing with graduate students in the bright, modern university building, in an atrium surrounded by skeletons of ancient monsters, discussing their connection with contemporary ones. That *something* had driven him all his life, and he couldn't stop searching just because he no longer had a job. So, he did the TV crypto thing, perpetuating false myths to get money to explore the real thing on his own time. No wife, no family. Plenty of infamy, but no real recognition. That cut deep. No, he had nothing but the unquenchable thirst of pursuit. He wished to hell he knew what he was pursuing.

The door behind him swished open, then clacked shut. Duff's wife, Mary, leaned on the railing, her sharp, dark eyes sizing him up. She had a cigarette in one hand and an old metal lighter in the other. He liked Mary. She was kind, calm, and nobody's fool. Certainly not Duff's.

"Supper's almost ready. You–"

She was interrupted by the honking of a goose flying low over the house, right above their heads. Duff's dogs were going nuts out back. Roger looked up. The goose's calls had a piercing edge that tugged at his guts. It vanished, honking into the dark, following the path the other geese had taken earlier. This time, the hairs on the nape of his neck stood at attention.

"Only one flying tonight, Mary?"

"Yup. It's a Goose Star night"—Mary's face had gathered into worry lines, and her cigarette trembled—"when only one ever flies, and he means trouble." She took a puff.

The night's heartbeat had quickened. Or was it Roger's own—too much beer after a day of exertion. He would be careful with the booze tonight, especially as the other men seemed two-thirds down the highway to Drunksville already.

Jason thrust the door wide. The odour of rum permeated the air around him. *Hell. How much had he downed in ten minutes?*

"Duff's got the food on the table," said Jason. He glared at Mary. "Let's eat. Now." He turned, slamming the door again.

"Shit," said Mary under her breath and stubbed out her smoke in the deck's ashtray.

"What?"

"Later."

○

Roger had just dropped a drunken Jason onto a bed in the guest cabin when someone knocked on the door. It was Mary, holding a brown paper bag and a thermos, a black eye blossoming where Jason had slugged her when she got in between him and Duff.

"Here's your dessert and decaf."

"Thanks." He rustled the bag open and peered in. Two pieces of apple pie with cheese. *All right.* "That eye looks awful. How are you feeling?"

"I won't deny it hurts, but I'm fine. Shocked, but fine."

"You pressing charges?"

"No. Too much trouble for what it's worth and I don't want to be dragging Duff into it. Duff avenged my honour sufficiently. Besides, life has a way of evening things up."

"I guess. How's Duff?"

"I just poured him into bed. Jason got the worst of it tonight, but Duff'll feel it more in the morning, the old fart."

"Is the shoot still on? Should we leave?"

"Duff was all for banning Jason from the property. But, frankly, you pay so well, I convinced him to let it continue. But Jason's got to sleep in town starting tomorrow, and you better keep him away from us. If you want to come back again after that, no Jason. But you're always welcome here, Roger." She patted his hand.

"Thanks, Mary. I appreciate it." He gave her hand a brief squeeze. "I guess Jason'll be sporting bruises for the camera. We'll have to work it into a night confrontation with something big and hairy in the bush."

Roger shifted his own complaining, Jason-hauling, upper back muscles. They'd been uncomfortable for days and this wouldn't make things better.

"Big and hairy. That's my Duff. So, we need to talk. About the goose."

"Okay." The goose had called while he half-dragged Jason home on the stony path down to the cabin. He'd asked Jason if he heard it, but Jason was passed out again. It was all Roger could do to slap some consciousness into him and get him moving. But *the something* had pulled at Roger the whole trek down, while wolves had howled in the distance, adding to his agitation.

"Let's talk on the bench outside. Out of earshot." She pointed at Jason.

"He's out for the night."

"Just in case." She pulled her jacket collar up. "Grab your coat and bring the coffee."

○

"You felt it, too," she said. Her hands wrapped around the steaming coffee mug. "When the Goose Star bird flew over."

The wind had risen, shaking the trees in the boreal forest surrounding the cabin, crackling dead aspen leaves clinging to branches, whispering through the grasses. The stars were harsh diamonds in a bleak sky. A single drift of thin, dark clouds shadowed the sickle moon. In the distance, a wolf howled with a wild single note, swooping up and ending in an ululation of urgency.

"What's the Goose Star?"

"Look up there, in the northern sky. You know the constellation, Cygnus?"

"The Swan? Yes, but I'm not sure which stars they are."

She pointed them out to him. "Could be a swan, a crane, a goose. Different bird around the world."

"But never a penguin."

She shook her head, then continued: "You see that star below the head?" She pointed again. "That's Anser. Around here, when Anser shines brightest, no other geese fly but one—the one you heard—the night goose."

Tonight, the star was the brightest damn thing around. The wolf howled again, raising Roger's own hackles. He pulled his jacket tighter. *Something...*

She continued, "Twice a year this happens, when the geese migrate, spring and fall. Local wisdom has it that their passing lifts the souls of all those who have died since the last migration, so the story goes. The calls awaken the souls and ready them for flight. Then the geese gather the souls as they pass. Freedom."

"Uh huh." Skepticism was the appropriate crapto-zoologist response. But...

A second wolf started up. In hysterical response, Duff's dogs barked and bugled.

"A night for hunting, I guess," said Mary.

The wind whipped Mary's dark grey hair around her face. She lit a cigarette, the bright tip a moving ember in the darkness. He shivered again. *The something* was abroad here in this place. Might as well just succumb to it. Once again, he was a child alone in the dark woods, listening to the pulse of the forest and hearing another beyond.

"So, what's the night goose about?

"Old Blue Eyes—because of the blue chin strap that goes right to his eyes, although the two Brit expats who run the grocery store call him Herne—he seeks the souls of those who have done grievous harm in this life. Huge, black wolfdogs are said to escort him—but no one's ever seen them. Lots of people have heard them, though."

"Sounds like a real hodgepodge of lore."

She shrugged. "All I can say is that's what we've seen around here. And we don't mess with it."

She took a long drag off her cigarette, letting the smoke out slowly, then continued: "He flies before dawn or after dusk, when the other geese sleep, and the regular souls have flown. He comes for the evil dead, not to free those souls, but to bind them."

Another drag, her eyes off to the horizon, in the direction of the wolf howls. Acid scraped Roger's stomach. The damn coffee. Still, he wanted to hear more. This story held possibilities for an episode. Mary stubbed out the butt and lit another.

She said, "If he senses such a one about, still alive, he'll hunt them down. If the person hears him before they're dead, he'll pull their soul so they can't do more harm. During the hunt, the Goose Star blazes until it's all over."

"And you think..."

"Yeah, he's after Jason. That boy's done very bad things, and he's going to do more."

Another wolf joined the chorus, then another, then a fifth, until the sound echoed off the hills, knifing through the wind.

"Jason needs help," he said. "Anger management. AA. Therapy. He's not evil, just lost."

"Then keep him from hearing the night goose. Get him that help."

"How am I supposed to do that?"

"That's all I know."

"Jason's already had two escapes tonight." He told her about the second call and Jason's lucky flight into oblivion on the walk.

"He may need a couple more escapes before you guys are done." Mary gulped down the last of her coffee, and handed him the cup. "I don't think Old Blue Eyes cares about second chances. He's all search and destroy. It's up to you now, Roger. Tell Jason, or don't tell Jason. Deal with it as you think best. Now get some sleep. You've got an early start tomorrow. Goodnight."

And she left. The spark of her cigarette danced through the blackness like an out-of-season firefly, while wolf howls swirled about her on the night wind.

○

"Hell, you sure you got enough cameras?" said Jason.

Roger had set them up himself that afternoon. It had been a struggle. The field stubble was uneven and slippery with goose scat.

"Yeah, yeah, I know. I want to catch as many angles as I can until I know what I'm going to do."

Two cameras were set for low-light shooting. Three others were infrared. He'd even unearthed a few instruments on poles from the back of his van that were meant to ring warning bells and capture ectoplasm on film. He'd won them in a poker game from Gustav, the *Ghost Safari* guy. Gus had said they were accurately calibrated. Calibrated against what real-life phenomenon Roger had no idea. Pure crap. But tonight, he'd try anything. And even if nothing happened, the devices would look cool onscreen.

Earlier that day, before dawn, the two men had gone hunting. Jason was again all for it, especially since Duff now refused to join them. Roger made sure they were in position long before the sun rose. He wanted to see if Old Blue Eyes would make a predawn strike at Jason. Supposedly to fill in the boring waiting period until dawn, Roger had given Jason noise-cancelling headphones and the job of authenticating a recording of Big Foot sounds. And yes—right on cue—the bird had buzzed Jason twice while completely ignoring Roger a few metres away. The bird was a big male, black but for the pale patches on its belly and chest. No white chin strap, but rather a bright blue one, as Mary had described. He could hear Duff's small pack of hunting dogs sounding in the distance. Then the goose vanished. Jason was oblivious to the whole thing and Roger didn't fill him in.

Roger had almost peed himself. The myth seemed to be real. The bird was paranormal, a true cryptid. It could be *the something* he had spent his life searching for.

"So, here's the plan, Jason. When the sun's setting, you put on the fur suit—the good one. Once you hear the geese coming to settle for the night, you go out into the field and lurch around. You know the Big Foot drill. I figure between the low light and the geese flying all around you, it'll be a nice, obscure shot."

"Then?"

"Pretend you notice us and run off, away from the cameras, over there to the edge of the field, under the trees. See that pile of rocks? Bang on some tree trunks with one."

"This part's not on film, right?"

"Well, yeah, it is, but we won't be able to see anything. Shake some bushes nice and loud. Then sneak back around here to me. Once the sun is down and the birds are gone—because I don't think they're going to hang around once they've seen us—then, we'll go into the fields with flashlights and a handheld, and show the crushed stubble where the creature stalked."

"Maybe I should go first and plant hair tufts as I go, like that time in British Columbia?"

"Great idea."

They sat at the edge of the field in sight of the cameras, a pair of watchful cryptozoologists on the prowl. *The something* flowed through Roger. Tonight, he'd see it again with his own eyes. Plus, he'd have the proof necessary to rebuild his reputation. Funding. No more chicanery. He could taste the honey-sweet redemption already.

Jason checked his cellphone while they waited.

"Huh. Looks like Sophie called. I told her earlier I was working tonight. I said only call if it's an emergency."

"Do you want to phone her back? We've got time and good cell reception."

"Nah, it's never an emergency. They can't find their socks, or they're lonely. Stupid shit like that."

"Who's watching them this weekend? Your sister?" Jason's children were a boy, Skyler, aged four, and a girl, Sophie, aged six.

"No. She's out of town, with the grandparents. Sophie can handle things, though."

"Wait. What if they cut or burn themselves?"

"I left them with plenty of cereal and milk, so they don't have to cook, and the TV works. I locked them in good."

"What if someone tries to break in? Is anyone checking on them?"

"Look, Roger, you're pissing me off. I love the little crappers. I truly do. They're the only reason I can get up some mornings. But they have to learn about life and how to stand on their own two feet. How I run my family is my business. Sophie knows what 911 is for."

"Call a sitter. Now. I'll pay for it. Don't they get scared? Christ, Jason, she's only six."

"Since when did you become an expert on six-year-olds, Mr. I-Never-Had-Any-Kids? They're smarter than people give them credit for. They're fine."

"Look, Jason–"

"That's enough, Roger, or so help me I'll knock your block off, boss or not. I know what I'm doing. The kids are fine. Subject is closed."

They sat in silence. Roger came to a decision.

"I guess you know what you're doing all right. Sorry for giving you a hard time."

Jason grunted. After a while, he said, "I appreciate that. No harm done."

Jason's thermos flask sips had turned into gulps. Roger knew it wasn't coffee, but for once said nothing. He tossed his decision back and forth, feeling ill and excited in turns. When Jason got to the spitting angry stage, muttering about how those kids of his had better toe the line or else, and cursing his dead wife for breaking his heart, Roger lost any qualms. He paused when he saw the tears in Jason's maudlin eyes, but then *the something* surged within him.

"Dammit, Roger, let's do it now," said Jason. "To hell with waiting for the stupid birds."

"Sure, Jason. Go ahead. And you know what? Forget about the earphones. The transmitter's not working properly. You know what you're doing."

"Damn right." Jason took off the earphones, lurched to his feet and set off.

The geese were on their way. Roger no longer asked himself how he knew. He made a hasty call to 911 once Jason was out of earshot.

Jason stumbled out into the middle of the field as the low sun in the orange sky sent the long shadows racing across the stubble. The trees at the edge turned dark, a wolf howled, and the wind dropped. Blocking the sun, Jason was nothing more than a shadow himself. He bent as if searching the ground for something, then lurched to a new spot. Lather. Rinse. Repeat. And then they came.

Skein upon skein of geese formed one vast wedge, raising their own wind. Their calls filled the air with sound and Roger with rapture. As they landed, Jason rose from a crouch. Alarmed, they lifted in a storm of frantic wings and flapped about him. Roger saw the ecto-poles begin a wild, shaking dance and their bells pinged and buzzed, metallic and piercing, even over the racket of the geese. Jason turned on cue to the cameras, still nothing but a shadow, and, beating at the birds around him, hightailed it to the field's edge.

Roger sank to the ground, his heart hammering as never before. He ignored the discomfort. His whole body burned, and he was drenched in sweat. He grinned as he waited for Jason. It wasn't over. *The something* was subdued, but it was still moving, restless, through the brush and over the field.

○

"Friggin' freezing, Roger." Jason's words were slurred. "Can we start now? Sun's already dropped. I can't wait to finish and wash the goddamn goose shit off me."

Roger, however, was still hot—feverish, nauseated, and filled with excitement.

The something whispered around Roger, calling to him. The heartbeat of the night pulsed through him, and far off, a single goose trumpeted. The darkness was complete. The wolves began their howling again, sending tingles up Roger's spine.

"Okay, sure, Jason. Let's head out into the field. I'll do the camera. You grab the flashlight and take the lead. Just ignore the wolves. They sound like they're miles away."

"Hell, yeah. I'm no bush greenhorn."

Jason sniggered as he staggered off ahead, planting and then exclaiming over tufts of bear-like fur in the broken stubble. Roger caught it all on camera, despite the pain shooting through his overworked arms. Jason was too drunk to be convincing, but that wasn't the point of this, was it?

The wolves were silent now and the goose calls were getting closer, Doppler-like, as the goose flew up to, and then passed the two men.

"Hell, that bird's fast," said Jason, shining his light upwards. The blue patches flashed. "Hey, it's coming back. Straight for me..."

Jason took off running as Old Blue Eyes dove in, his shrill calls building, their edges sharpening, relentless as a train whistle. Roger aimed the camera at Jason and the bird and kept pace as best he could with his pounding heart and panting breath. Adrenaline pushed him onward faster than he would have dreamed. The ecto-bells pinged madly as Jason and the bird passed by. Luckily Jason kept to a path the cameras could follow.

Then, Jason tripped, yelling, and the goose hovered like a giant hummingbird. A scream, then silence. A faint, writhing blue rendition of Jason appeared and churned through the air above his body. Old Blue Eyes, lit by the tossed flashlight, snagged a wisp of blue ecto-Jason with a claw, and pulled it away, up into the air, vanishing with a final, echoing honk. Wolves howled jubilantly, then ceased, an eerie silence in their wake.

Roger sagged to the ground beside Jason's slumped body, laid down the heavy camera, balanced the flashlight on his knees, and checked Jason's throat for a pulse. Nothing. Roger's arms were sore. Pain radiated from his shoulders. His breath came in great, struggling heaves. Maybe he was sorry for Jason, but the thing felt right. The face of Jason's late wife flashed in his mind. Those kids would be better off with their grandparents. The man's time had come, clearly, and when a man's time came, there was nothing to stop it.

Roger's heart leaped to his throat. Sweat rolled down his back. It was done. Over. Jason's kids would be safe, and his reward would be grasping the mystical *something*. His lifelong hunt had ended.

He had *seen* it. With his own eyes. What's more, he had filmed it with two kinds of camera. He had records of activity from the ecto-poles. He knew the television people would never play it, showing as it did a death. But the scientific community would be won over. They would subject the measures to all kinds of tests for verification, but it was the *truth* so it would all hold up—right? His heart danced and shuddered in his chest. His elation grew as *the something* blossomed in every cell of his being, connecting him to the universe in a way nothing, no drug, no person, had ever done for him.

A rustling came from the far side of the field, then, hesitant honks. He looked up. The Goose Star had dimmed. Roger's whole world narrowed to his happiness and the growing blaze in his heart and lungs. The geese rose by waves into the sky until once again the world resounded with their wild bugling. He thought he would burst with exultation. If only he could breathe. He gasped, struggling against the crushing agony in his chest that warred with the joy. Joy won. The pain left. The birds surrounded him, circling gently; their powerful wings shoved the cameras off kilter. They fluttered him in a drift of feathers, not touching him, waiting. They lifted him with their song of longing. They filled him with wonder and terror until he was gone, and freed, and the cameras died in the cold, deep, darkness of the night, with nothing on the audio tracks but the sudden thunder of a single heartbeat.

At least it was *something.*

BLOODBATH
(VHS, 1987, DIRECTOR UNKNOWN)

David Demchuk

"I found something you two might like," Ted said to Lana, pointing to one of the plastic clamshell video cases on his display table, nestled alongside a trio of Lucio Fulcis with their original Italian cover art.

Ted was big and bald, with red suspenders over a blue and black plaid shirt, probably pushing fifty. He knew Lana, knew both of us, from our flea market visits three or four times a year. We weren't his biggest customers, but he genuinely seemed to like us in a non-creepy way and always shone a big grin when he found something for us that we hadn't seen.

"Hey, Jenny, do you remember this?" she asked me as she reached over and picked up the case.

BLOODBATH, it shrieked across the cover in cartoony letters reminiscent of, well, blood. Below it, what looked like a snapshot of maimed and mutilated bodies lined up along the walls in the corner of someone's cellar. Black blotches where their eyes had been. "I don't know," I answered. "Maybe?"

"I do," she said, turning the case over to scan the back. "The rental place at the mall had it mixed in with a bunch of old Hammer movies and *Friday the 13th* ripoffs. It was never in when I asked though, or so they said. Maybe I was too young." A prominent yellow box in the lower corner said "18+."

The hall wasn't even half full and already the crowd was overwhelming me. I inched closer to the display table, took the case from Lana. *A family reunion turns into a night of screaming horror.* I did remember it, actually, though I wasn't sure from where. My cousin Lana and I grew up at opposite ends of town, went to different schools (West Kildonan vs. Daniel Mac), different shopping centres (Garden City vs. Polo Park), and of course different video stores, so there must've been a few copies around town. Lana was a devoted horror fan, but she was limited by what her mother would let into the house. I, on the other hand, had been obsessed for as long as I could remember, first with fairy tales, comic books and movie magazines, then with trashy drugstore paperbacks and late-night creature features, and finally with the high-grade heroin of Frankie's Movie Wall.

Frankie's had been a few blocks from DMCI, and his titular movie wall was dominated mainly by slashers and porn. *Humongous*, *April Fool's Day*, *Rituals*, *Silent Scream*, *The Beast Within* and *Tourist Trap* on the lower shelves, and glossy pink cardboard boxes up above, adorned with pouty lingerie-clad blondes. Had I seen the box for *BLOODBATH* at Frankie's? I wasn't sure. He hadn't cared what I rented, and neither had my foster parents, as long as I kept the sound down while they were trying to sleep. So maybe I did bring it home one night and just forgot? I handed it back to her.

"Ten bucks," Ted said as Lana tugged the case open.

"Seriously?" Lana asked. "This movie didn't cost ten bucks to make."

Ted shrugged. Her eyes shifted towards me.

"Don't even ask," I said.

I'd been let go from my waitressing job a few days before so my asshole boss Rick the Prick could use my salary to go to Disneyland with his horrible wife and kids. Lana had taken me to an afternoon showing of *Saw II* to cheer me up and then brought me to the flea, but all it did was remind me of everything I couldn't afford.

I peered over her shoulder. The cassette inside looked suitably beaten-up; more like a homemade dub than a real factory-pressed video. Little shreds of sticky paper clung along one edge where a label had once been.

"Come on, Rick," she said. "How is this ten bucks? It looks like it was made in somebody's basement."

He turned his eyes back to the years-old issue of *Penthouse Forum* he held up to his face like a dare.

"Ugh. Fine," I said to Lana, and pulled a five out of my wallet. She matched it with one of her own, then handed the bills over.

"Have you seen it?" I asked him. "Is it any good?"

"I don't watch this shit," he said. "I just sell it. I have enough stress in my life."

○

Lana moved aside another box in her storage room and uncovered the Goldstar VHS player on the lowest shelf on the back wall. She lifted it up and out while I reached over and tugged on the power cord and AV cords from where they had fallen behind.

"This is a lot of work for a crappy-ass video that probably isn't even scary," I said.

The dust on the player was so thick that it was clouding up in puffs around my arms and face.

I hadn't really known Lana until I was eight or nine, a few years after the accident that left me in the care of a pleasant but not especially affectionate foster family. I decided at the time that they were reluctant to develop any real feelings for me in case someone showed up to adopt me, but no one ever did. My father's family was distant and estranged, and my mother's only sister, Aunt Lila, was overburdened as a single mom with two daughters of her own.

Still, I did get to see them once or twice a month, usually for dinners downtown at Sammy's, a warm woody 'family restaurant' on Donald Street with a waving sandwich made of neon on the sign above the door and a buffet in the next room that was too expensive for us. "We're not made of money," Lila would say to her oldest daughter, Evelyn, a surly teenager who often acted as if she'd been forced to sit among strangers. Evelyn was turning sixteen and acted like I had rabies, while Lana was only three years older than me and treated me like a long lost kid sister from the moment we met. The four of us got along well enough, and I could see how tight things were for them and the struggles they were facing; still, I was convinced that they didn't take me in because I was damaged goods and more trouble than I was worth.

"Why can't I come live with you?" I asked Lila once in the parking lot while she was lighting her cigarette. The girls were still inside the restaurant, in the washroom, because they had bladders as big as peas.

Lila paused for a moment, drew a great gust of smoke into her lungs, then let it out in a plume up into the cool evening air. "Oh honey, I wish you could, but it's just not possible. Not now, anyway. Maybe someday, fingers crossed." Then she looked over at me, and really looked at me, right into my eyes so we could each see the other's sadness. "Are they all right? The Voloshyns? Are they treating you okay?" I nodded. "Good. They knew your mother. I mean, they met once or twice, years ago. We all knew each other back then."

Funny they never mentioned it, I thought. Just then the door burst open and Lana and Evelyn came out, laughing and joking about one of their teachers. Lila sighed, ground her cigarette into the ground and hustled us into the car.

○

Lana carried the VCR up from the basement back to her apartment on the third floor while I followed behind her holding my breath. She set it down on the coffee table, plugged it into the extension cord snaked behind her entertainment stand. The little red power light flashed on in its smoky front window, and a whirring churning sound came from within. She pushed its red, yellow and white plugs into the side of the TV, and I switched modes until I found the one with the angular VCR1 letters floating tremulously in the upper left corner.

I flopped myself into the armchair while she popped into the kitchen and came back with the big bags of Old Dutch Rip-L Chips and the giant bottle of Pic-a-Pop Cream Soda that I'd insisted on, touchstones of my nutritionally challenged childhood.

"Ready?" I asked, as she poured me a large glass of fizzy fluorescent pinkness and seated herself on the couch.

She nodded, pulled open one of the bags, and emptied it into a large metal bowl she'd pulled out from under the kitchen counter.

I took the cassette and slid it into the front of the machine, felt it engage with the workings inside. The picture on the TV snapped to life and a whining wave of tracking lines soared up from the bottom of the screen. The bright red word *BLOODBATH* faded into the centre, a faint haze around it hinting at the recording's illicit origins. I took a sip from the soda, the cotton-candy fullness flooding my mouth. Once again the screen—and the room—were plunged into darkness. No credits, no music. And then the first image sprang up, flat and grey and cold.

A house, two storeys, clapboard siding, gabled roof; lights on along the front and side of the first floor. The porch light glows in the darkness, searing the camera's lens.

"Oh gross," Lana cried, "it was shot on video! These movies are never scary."

Nighttime sounds, crickets and whistling wind, the occasional peeping frog. After a few moments, the basement light at the far right switches on. Sombre shadows move back and forth inside the ground-level window, hands and heads and arms.

She sighed and then stuffed a fistful of chips into her mouth. *Crunch crunch.* I shushed her and continued to watch. She was right though: The flatness of the image reminded me of the bland cheap look of daytime soap operas, CKND's late-night local news broadcasts, and the VPW cable access shows of my childhood like *Pollock and Pollock's Gossip Show* and *Chmielewski Fun Time* which Lana and I had watched with horrified fascination. Still, the photo on the front of the case intrigued me, and always had, so I continued to hold out some hope.

Abruptly, the image moves: Someone is holding the camera, and they slowly and cautiously approach the house. In one long shot, the viewer creeps in among the cars parked in the driveway, carefully steps up to the front porch, pushes the front door open. Only then do we realize that the viewer is someone quite short, possibly even a child. The frame floods with light and then adjusts; the ceiling light and floor lamps leaving bright traces across the screen. The viewer moves into the living room with its velvet tufted couch, matching armchair, occasional table, swag lamp, shag carpet.

"Was this shot somewhere around here?" I asked. "It looks familiar."

"Maybe," Lana replied, crunching more chips.

It could have been a seat-of-your-pants production by some long-forgotten local auteur. That would explain why none of my video horror guides ever mentioned it.

The viewer continues on through the dining room with its china cabinet and walnut table and chairs, then turns into the kitchen furnished with avocado and gold appliances. Finally, the camera dips unsteadily and then wheels around toward the door that leads to the basement stairs. From behind it we hear the faraway sounds of chanting, and urgent muffled screams.

"Holy shit, it's found footage," Lana whispered. "I wonder if the *Blair Witch* guys saw this."

I sighed. This was unlikely to be some obscure foundational masterwork. *Cannibal Holocaust* was more or less the first found-footage horror movie, released in 1980, years before this. And *Black Christmas* had started with the killer-tracking-around-the house trope back in the 1970s. Still, props to whomever for their unaffected stab at no-budget vérité.

I took another swallow of the cream soda, which had an oddly bitter undertaste, and then sat back in my chair. Was this really the beginning of the film? Did we miss a whole hour of plot and character? Or was this some kind of extended flashback? We hadn't really been anywhere and it was starting to seem like there was nowhere for us to go.

A small hand shoots out from beside the camera, grabs the faceted glass doorknob and gives it a sharp twist and pull. The basement door springs open, and the sounds from below are suddenly louder and more distinct. The viewer steps into the stairwell, and an older woman, pasty and naked, her lips a slash of crimson, leers into view. She gestures for the viewer to move past her on the stairs. "Go on then," she says, and the viewer obeys. An older naked man, his face powdered and painted, draws in his belly to let the viewer by. Two more old people stand at the bottom of the stairs and smile encouragingly. A piercing shriek from the right, and the camera scans past a cluttered workbench and a shadowy pantry to stop on a trio of robed, hooded officiants, facing what seems to be a family of five who are tied and gagged and kneeling, shaking with terror, against the basement's far wall.

"Okay, this is very fucked up," I said, unsure of what I was seeing.

My first thought, an impossible thought, was that what we were watching was real. I took another long sip of my drink, and Lana noisily opened the second bag of chips.

"I can see why the guy in the mall would never rent it to me," she replied. "That old guy in the corner definitely has a hard-on."

One of the officiants, tall and thin, face shadowed by the hood of their robe, moves forward and grabs the hair of the first family member—a round old woman in a flowered housedress spattered with blood and muck. The officiant pulls the old woman's head back, holds up a small scythe-like blade and brings it down into her eye socket. The old woman lets out a horrible shriek as the officiant swiftly circles the inside of the socket—scoops out the eye—and drops it into a nearby metal bowl. "She likes the soft parts first," someone moans off-camera. The officiant sinks the blade into the second socket, swirls it around, pushes up slightly to lift the eyeball free, then once again pulls it out and drops into the bowl. The other family members wail and writhe but the old woman is motionless, overcome with pain and shock. The officiant slides the bowl over in front of the next family member, a heavier middle-aged man in a wide-collared plaid sport shirt and navy trousers—perhaps the old woman's son. He struggles furiously against the rope and gag, but it's useless. He is tightly bound and cannot pull himself free. He watches helplessly as the officiant leans in, blade at the ready.

"This is so fake," Lana said, through a mouthful of chips. "You can buy those rubber eye things at the novelty shop. Just watch if they drop one and see if it bounces."

For the first time in years, I was genuinely uncomfortable, sickened even, watching something I knew couldn't be true. I had giggled and snacked my way through scores of decapitations, mutilations, disembowelings and devourings, some more realistic than others. But something about this was landing too hard with me. I felt lightheaded; my breathing rapid and shallow. I picked up the glass and finished the last of the pop, then felt it lurch as it landed in the pit of my stomach. Bad idea.

Lana looked over at me. "Hey Jen, are you okay?" she asked,

as another wave of screeching tore out of the TV's speakers. The neighbours would be pounding on the door any minute.

The officiant drops the man's left eye into the bowl, then returns to remove the second. The man thrashes back and forth, spraying blood everywhere. The officiant grabs him by the hair and slams his head against the stone wall, once, twice. The thrashing stops. The officiant makes quick work of the second eye while the bound and gagged woman next to him turns her head away, wincing and whimpering. "What about the tongues?" someone asks off-screen, somewhere behind the chanting figures. "The tongues can wait," another voice answers, older and deeper. "The eyes come first."

"I think I need to lie down," I said.

The room was starting to tilt and spin. I stretched myself out on the couch and rested my head on the needlepoint pillow leaning against the armrest.

"You had those disgusting corn dogs, you brought it on yourself," she sighed. "It's okay, Lila's going to come by soon and take me back to her place. You just rest while I finish."

I closed my eyes for a moment, then opened them again slightly to glance at the screen. Lana was watching intently, tapping the last of the chips out of the bag.

The woman, likely the wife of the man and the mother of the children, lets out a high keening sound as the officiant takes her by her hair, then the sound climbs to an even higher pitch as the blade plunges into her flesh and begins to carve. Her cries abruptly drop into a soft gasping whine as first one eye, and then the other, are quickly removed and dropped into the bowl. The officiant pushes her back against the wall, blood washing down her cheeks, and shifts over to the teenaged boy next to her, presumably her son.

I closed my eyes again, still queasy and dizzy, the sticky-sweet soda climbing up the back of my throat and stinging like acid. Why did this seem so real to me, when Lana found the whole thing so hokey and laughable?

The boy starts to flail back and forth but the officiant pulls his head forward, plunges the blade into the back of his neck and twists it. His face fills with terror as his body goes completely limp. One eye, then the other, are swiftly removed and placed in the bowl, and the officiant—and the viewer—turn to face a very young blonde girl in flower-patterned overalls.

"I think we should stop now," I rasped.

Could it be the cream soda? But why wasn't Lana feeling sick? Her lips were moving soundlessly as she watched, synchronized with the chanting of the people in the basement. I could catch a word here and there, but none of it made any sense.

The viewer moves in to watch closely as the officiant unties the child and leads her away from the carnage, then returns to the bowl, picks it up, turns and steps to the edge of the uncovered sewer hole in the centre of the floor. Dozens of delicate lizard-like tongues, long and lithe, wave and stretch from inside it, reaching instinctively for the officiant. They run all over the officiant's face and robe and legs, leaving tiny wounds and traces of blood in their wake.

Nearby, another officiant crouches down to face the cowering child, takes her shoulders in her hands. "You belong with us now," she says, then turns her to face the tongues in the sewer. They watch together as the first officiant empties the bowl into the hole, tosses it aside with a clang, then lets the tongues wrap around her limbs and waist and throat, thrust through her flesh, into her ribs and chest and under her robe, then pull her off her feet and down into the sewer.

Then one of the officiants turns to the camera and says, clear as a bell: "You can turn it off now, Evelyn." And the image snaps into shrill hissing static.

"Wow, that tongue monster, amazing," Lana said. "I wonder how they did that."

She looked over at me as another wave of buzzing tracking lines traversed the screen. My eyelids fluttered as I began to sink deep into myself, and I heard her ask from what seemed like a mile away: "It was good that Ted found that video, wasn't it?"

And then softer, closer, like a feather teasing my ear: "Jenny. Have you ever heard of the *Naystarsha*?"

○

I have no real memory of my family's deaths. I should, and sometimes I pretend I do. What I do remember is mostly what other people said when I was younger, and what I said back to them, in a weird game of broken telephone. At night, in the dark and the quiet, I try to take myself back, to picture any of it, to see a real image, hear a real sound. Nothing. I mentioned it to a friend in first year once and she said it was probably trauma and that I should see a counsellor or a psychologist. "The school has some people," she had said, though she thought they were mostly student volunteers, and to me that felt too much like getting a root canal at the School of Dentistry.

What I was told: We were in the car coming back from my dad's birthday dinner at The Happy Vineyard and were about to drop off my grandmother at the seniors' home when we were T-boned at an intersection and crushed against a concrete utility pole. My parents, in the front seats, were killed instantly. My brother and grandmother died on the way to the hospital. I had fussed with my seatbelt earlier and unclasped it along the way. I was thrown out the side door and into a ditch, soft and wet with cattails and rainwater. I ended up with some cuts and bruises and a concussion, and my right arm was broken in two places, but somehow I survived.

My foster parents refused to tell me anything about the accident, or even about my family apart from their names and ages. They didn't know what my parents were like, and they didn't want to know. So the first people to tell me anything about them were Aunt Lila and cousin Lana.

One time at the movies, I took Lana aside and asked her what had happened. She wasn't supposed to tell me, she said, and then promptly divulged everything. I had nightmares that night, and for several nights after, but I loved her for telling me and resented everyone else for keeping my life a secret from me. While I still couldn't picture the accident itself, I could imagine it using scenes and moments from movies like *Race with the Devil, Maximum Overdrive, Carnival of Souls* and *Duel*, and then finally the climactic burst of telekinesis in *Carrie*, where she flings an oncoming vehicle out of the way, rolls it over and makes it explode.

This last image struck me so deeply that I wondered if I had caused the accident myself.

A few years later, when I was twelve or so, I was with Lana at the library when I asked the tiny old woman behind the counter if she could look up an obituary for me on the microfiche. Lana pulled me aside. "There hadn't been one," she had whispered, because obituaries cost money, and my father's life insurance had barely covered my family's cremation. Aunt Lila had emptied the apartment herself, had taken care of the estate, and had paid hundreds in lawyer's fees and taxes. My family's ashes were interred at a small cemetery out near Headingley where she had been able to get a good deal. If I wanted to go, Lana would check to see if there was a bus we could take, but it was better not to mention it to Aunt Lila as it would hurt her feelings. She would see it as me yearning for a connection with people who were dead and gone, who I had barely known and couldn't remember, instead of with those I had now, who were alive and right here in front of me. I had nodded. I would never do anything to hurt Aunt Lila, who had done so much to help me. I had told Lana I'd never mention it again, and I never did.

Instead, I treated the hole in my memory like a very still, very deep pond, with a weathered wooden fence around it, in a garden in the centre of my mind. I could climb over the fence and kneel at the edge, I could decorate it with dark sad fantasies, I could dip my hand into the cool clear water, but I could never do more—for fear that I might fall in and drown, or that something might reach up for me, take hold of me, and pull me in.

○

All this to say I slept, perhaps better than I ever had, with no tossing and turning, no early hour waking, no midnight glass of milk. I did dream though: Shadows upon shadows circling around me, dark blurry hands hovering over me, the rustling of cloaks and the scraping of shoes, a delicate caress on my cheek, and then a voice breathing into my ear.

You belong with us now.

A shiver ran through me like an electrical charge, up from the depths of my gut into my dry tight throat, a scream I stifled with both my hands. I bolted up from where I slept, reached out into the room's heavy blackness, tried to stand, then fell, fell to the floor, gasping and sobbing. That voice—that voice. That voice had belonged to Aunt Lila.

Gradually my eyes adjusted and I could pick out the shape of the room and its contents. I wasn't in my bedroom. I wasn't in Lana's apartment. In an instant I realized I was in the living room from the house in the video. It wasn't identical—the old armchair had been replaced with a leather-ish La-Z-Boy and the couch I'd been sleeping on had a souvenir blanket from Niagara Falls tossed over it. But the shag rug was the same, the spun-plastic swag lamp and drapes were the same. From somewhere below, I could hear the low drone of a harmonium, the jangle of a bandura, and voices caught up in chatter.

A table lamp snapped on in the corner of the room. I looked

past the stinging glare of the light to see Aunt Lila sitting there, smoking, watching me.

"I'm sorry that you found out like this," she said. "It's not what I had planned. But the Oldest Ones have Their ways in the world, and we cannot comprehend them."

"Where am I?" I asked. My tongue felt thick and lazy, barely capable of forming words.

"Lana is their instrument," she continued, ignoring my question. "She knew what that tape was the moment she saw it, she knew it was meant for you. She thought it was the *Naystarsha* reaching out for you, making Herself known. A sign that at last it was time to draw back the curtain." She tapped the ash off her cigarette into a green glass bowl she held in her lap.

"You murdered my family," I said, still unable to replace the 'accident' that I'd been told of all my life with what I had seen on the video. "And now you're going to murder me."

"Jenny, please. That tape doesn't tell you everything. Your father was trying to undo our Order, to stop the emergence of the *Naystarsha*, all of our preparation, all of our plans. Decades we have been harbouring Her, sheltering Her. Centuries really. Moving Her from country to country to city to town, concealing Her, feeding Her, as She needs to be fed. He planned to expose us, to have us destroyed. To have *Her* destroyed. We couldn't allow it. And so, instead of a family of strangers, as we have always selected, we were forced to choose yours."

She raised the cigarette, drew in more smoke, held it, and then exhaled.

"We did maintain our traditions in one respect," she added. "Where there is a daughter and where she is the youngest, so she is spared. She is raised apart, she is nurtured and cared for, until the time is right. And then, one day, she is offered a choice. I hope you choose well, Jenny. As I said all those years ago, you belong with us now. And finally, here you are."

This has happened to her, I realized. *They sacrificed her family, but someone chose her to live, and she in turn chose me.*

"We have a word, *Akusherka,*" she continued. "A midwife, to the *Naystarsha*. When my turn comes to descend, you would take on this role. It comes with a modest allowance from our benefactors in the First Land, as well as some more unusual benefits. Evelyn is no longer a worry—she tried to part with us, and she paid the price. But Lana will need to be cared for, and for this I turn to you. I see how you are with each other. I would ask that you keep her close and help her as you can. It would be her honour to be your companion."

"What if I say no?" I rasped.

"No to Lana?" A tear welled at the corner of her eye. The sight of it enraged me.

"No to all of this," I gestured. "No to everything!"

"Then your time with us comes to an unfortunate end," she replied, tapping the ash in the bowl. "I can assure you it will be swift and free of pain."

"What if I killed you now?" I asked, my voice louder, harder, clearer. "I'm younger than you, and stronger."

"My dear, you can try, but you will not succeed. There is only One who can end my life now, and you have seen on the tape how She will do it." A rueful smile curled her lips. "It made us a little money, that tape, and it brought us a little following."

Suddenly, the thin trickle of music from below us stopped, and the sharp jagged chanting began.

"Ach, we are late, I always talk too much."

Lila stubbed out her cigarette and pushed herself up from her chair.

"The rituals mean nothing to the *Naystarsha*, She has no need for songs or dancing. But the participants find meaning in them, and that's what matters most. We all want to feel like our efforts have a purpose."

She set the green glass bowl, still smouldering, onto the small side table.

"I believe you know the Evanses, the husband was your employer. Not the most pleasant people, but much improved with the addition of some scopolamine patches and a few well-placed gags."

Lila stepped forward, reached out her hand to me. I had barely noticed, she had picked up a brown-paper sack as she rose, and now held it out to me. I could see the soft folds of the ceremonial robe tucked within it.

"Come. Lana is downstairs waiting with the camera. She is eager to see you make your debut. A lovely moment for you both to share." She stood there, watching, waiting. "Are you ready?"

A strange calm settled over me, and I realized that, yes, I was ready. I was. I had been since those first blurry images wobbled and shivered on Lana's TV screen. At last I felt like I was welcome and cared for, like I belonged. For the first time, I felt chosen.

The viewer watches from below as the two women, one older, one younger, robed and regal, step carefully down the staircase into the basement where a dazed and frightened family, drugged and pliant, huddle with their heads bowed. The two women take their hands, lead them past naked, chanting adherents, past the other robed officiants, taking them to the far stone wall, and pushing them to their knees. A fearful middle-aged man, his stoic wife, their confused and anxious trio of boys—a ten-year-old and two youngsters, close in age, possibly twins. The novice hands the older officiant the blade and the bowl and then steps back. "She likes the soft parts first," an elderly voice proclaims from off in the corner. The viewer observes as the older officiant moves to the husband, holds the glinting blade above his cheek, brings it down into the flesh and digs it deep into the socket, scraping against the bone.

The viewer turns away, looks to the newest novice, who now stands beside her, tears streaming down her face. "Shhh, it's okay," the viewer whispers to the novice from behind the camera. "You're here with us now." The lens glances down between them as their two hands clasp together. One hand tenderly squeezes the other as, from across the shadowed room, the screaming starts.

"I'm just..." The novice stops, sighs. "I'm just... so happy."

FRANK 2.0

Bob Armstrong

A Christmas party of some sort, Frank Milovic was sure of that much. But was it social or work, Helene's office party or his at… the newspaper? Yes. The *Edmonton Journal.* Where he edited the weekend book review and homes sections. Where he'd worked full-time for twenty-five years. It must be the *Journal's* annual seasonal celebration. That's what he'd gone to the closet for: to dress for the occasion.

That meant the Hugo Boss ready-to-wear suit he'd bought on sale at The Bay a few years before. But where was it? He looked for something familiar, like a stargazer getting his bearings by locating the Big Dipper. He called out for assistance.

"Helene, did you move my Oilers and Eskimos jerseys?"

"What?"

"I just noticed that they're missing."

"Didn't you take them to Goodwill years ago?"

As he opened his mouth to respond to this absurd suggestion, he was struck by the immensity and opulence of the closet. It was a walk-in and he must have been ten feet deep in it, with rows of clothing to the right and left. Shirts and sweaters and pants on one side. Suits and sport coats on the other. A tuxedo. Who owns his own tuxedo?

Clearly, this was not Frank's house. He was, for some reason, looking through the closet of a wealthy friend. Maybe he and Helene were housesitting. And he was experiencing short-term memory lapses. This was alarming, but not completely unexpected, as his father had died of Alzheimer's and in the years of his decline would often forget where he was. Frank would have to discuss this with Helene, but before alarming her, he'd get an opinion from his doctor. Maybe there was a less ominous explanation.

He turned to see Helene standing at the entrance to the closet, wearing a silk kimono and a bemused expression.

"Since when did you agonize over dressing for a party at Gregory's?"

Helene's hair was still up from the bath, but something was different about it. She'd obviously started using some new skin cream. And her teeth. So white. What was with her teeth?

"Hello? Frank? Are you okay?"

"Oh, just thinking about the party."

"It's not your rain pain, is it?"

Rain pain?

Helene placed a hand on Frank's left buttock and pressed, then continued palpating down the back of his thigh.

"Any tenderness there?"

"No. Fine."

What was she doing? And why did it seem she'd done this before? "Just lots on my mind, with work and Christmas. I can't seem to decide what to wear."

Helene reached into the closet and pulled out a casual hounds-tooth sport coat, a patterned violet shirt and a pair of navy blue slacks. "Try this. Now give me twenty minutes."

After Helene left the closet, Frank dropped his pants and turned to look at his buttocks and thigh in the mirror on the back wall. Where did that long scar come from? No answer was forthcoming, but the word "Peru" hovered on the horizon of his cognition. He stepped out of the closet and changed into the outfit Helene had selected and smiled at her as he left the bedroom to wander through his mysterious friend's house.

Frank tried to recall whose house it was. The director of Helene's clinic had a beautiful old place in Glenora, but it was nothing like this. The master bedroom led to a sitting room that offered a sentry's view of the great room, a high-ceilinged space dominated by an eight-foot-wide granite fireplace where Frank was sure he had kindled fires on more than one occasion. Beyond the fireplace stood a dining-room table which, even from this distance, Frank could tell was a one-of-a-kind handmade piece, with legs carved from salvaged oak beams. He descended the curving staircase to inspect the ground floor. African ceremonial masks, illuminated, hand-printed landscape photos and Latin American folk art adorned the walls and tables. An upright piano stood against one wall of the main room. Frank noted the sheet music in the stand above the keyboard: his favourite Christmas song, the Pogues' *Fairytale of New York.*

Every wine mom on Facebook was sharing memes with the slogan "Buy experiences, not things." But, Jesus Christ, Frank thought, wouldn't it be great to have the experience of owning things like this? And even if Frank's unknown host was a bit extravagant, the more he learned about the guy, the more he appreciated his taste.

Frank's path led to a closed door off a short hallway. As he gripped the brass doorknob, he knew this to be the owner's study. It was a working space. An old dining-room table served as a desk, piled with books arrayed in a semi-circle around a laptop. Heavy reading: three volumes of the papers of Theodore Roosevelt, a biography of Alexander von Humboldt, an illustrated volume on the making of Werner Herzog's *Aguirre: Wrath of God*, a world atlas from 1902, field guides to the birds, trees, reptiles, amphibians, mammals and insects of the Amazon Basin. To the right and left of the computer: two empty coffee cups, their bottoms stained by their dehydrated contents. Spilling out of the wastepaper basket: an array of printed pages with red-pen edits and additions in the margins.

Frank glanced at the closest shelf. Formative reading, sentimental favourites. Paperback editions he remembered from

English lit classes: Dickens and George Eliot, Naipaul and Richler, Dostoyevsky and Zola, Signet Classics editions of Shakespeare. A selection of obvious twentieth-century names from the British Isles: Orwell, Graham Greene, Burgess, the Amises, McEwan. A similar selection of Americans: Faulkner and Hemingway, Denis Johnson and Cormac McCarthy. Several shelves of Latin American writers, some of whom the owner had apparently read in Spanish. It was mostly an embarrassingly white and male collection, but there were a few more recent women added to the mix: Rachel Kushner and Jennifer Egan and Zadie Smith. Another set of shelves contained multiple copies of the same eight or ten books, their titles in English, French, German, Polish, Italian, Dutch, Spanish, and what Frank assumed must be Turkish. When he made out the name of the author of these works he spun on his heel and left the room and drank down a glass of water and stared at his face in a main floor bathroom mirror.

He needed to do something, needed to occupy himself while waiting for Helene. He would go out, warm up the car, clear the snow from the driveway. He walked to the foyer, reached into the large cut-glass bowl where somehow he knew the car keys were stored and stepped outside and realized the car would need no warming. There was a palm tree on his friend's yard. When, exactly, had Frank and Helene boarded an airplane? Running through the events of the previous several days in his head, he failed to notice Helene's approach.

"I'm looking forward to seeing the renovations," Helene said. "I haven't seen their house since Gregory had that dinner for Miguel."

Frank turned and saw Helene decked out in a party dress he'd never cast eyes on, wearing a chunky necklace of what looked like lapus lazuli. She was an attractive woman, and had aged better than Frank had, but suddenly she looked *hot*. He tried to conjure up an image of Gregory's house and handed the keys to Helene.

"I *am* a little under the weather. Do you think you could drive?"

Helene narrowed her eyes at him and took the keys and Frank followed her to the BMW in the garage. As Frank settled into the passenger seat and put geographic clues together, Helene glanced his way.

"I don't mind driving, so long as this doesn't mean you're going to raid Gregory's wine cellar. You know how Gregory loves to show it off."

Frank turned to Helene. "Of course not. I'm just—"

She placed a hand on his forehead and gave his reflection in the rearview an appraising look.

"You *do* look pale. And you were so excited about tonight. God, when you told me Gregory had signed Cormac McCarthy you squealed like Melissa at that One Direction concert."

Cormac McCarthy?

"Did not."

As Helene drove through streets she appeared to know too well, Frank saw himself rereading *Blood Meridian*, walking around the big house and reciting bits of flamboyant prose to Helene. Oh Christ.

But this was absurd. McCarthy's famously reclusive. He's not going to fly to some party in—judging by the licence plates on display—California. Frank grabbed his right cheek and gave it a hard pinch. Still in the BMW, approaching what a road sign insisted was the Bay Bridge, en route to San Francisco.

The route to Gregory and Miguel's became increasingly familiar as Helene negotiated I-80 traffic, turned on Market and climbed up to the Castro. They found parking at the bottom of a row of Victorian townhouses and ascended the steep sidewalk together to the uppermost house. Frank knocked on the heavy oaken door and it was opened by a smiling young woman who appeared to know him.

Hailey. The new office assistant. I should not know that.

"Mr. Milovic and Mrs. Milovic. Welcome! Happy Holidays! I'll tell Gregory you're here."

Voices already resounded around the house. Somewhere, a guitarist played a Latin-jazz version of *Have Yourself a Merry Little Christmas*. Glasses clinked. A distant blender mixed margaritas or daiquiris.

Two forty-something men appeared in the foyer: one thin with Julian Assange hair, the other broad-shouldered, dark and bearded.

The thin one stepped forward. "Frank! Helene! I'm so pleased you could come."

"Glad to be here," Frank offered.

Helene and the host exchanged air kisses. "You know, Gregory, Frank wouldn't have missed it for the world. We just told Melissa and Josh we'll meet them in Jackson on Monday."

Jackson? We can't afford to go to—

Frank saw himself launch into Corbett's Couloir and carve long powder turns down Rendezvous Mountain.

Never mind.

The bulky, dark one stepped forward to kiss Helene and shake Frank's hand.

"We are so pleased to share in another special occasion with you both. This has been a special year for us all. As if the universe were lining up for us."

Gregory and Miguel led Frank and Helene into the party and Frank made out familiar faces. Familiar from real life or from book jackets? There was Dave Eggers. There was Michael Chabon. Jennifer Egan and Rachel Kushner. Christ, was that Lena Dunham talking to Ta-Nehisi Coates?

The house was exquisite. Frank noticed that Gregory actually owned two adjoining row houses and had removed the dividing wall. That must cost a fortune, given San Francisco real estate prices. Then again, if Gregory represented all these people, he could afford it.

Helene had mentioned renovations. Frank supposed that he was expected to know what the house looked like previously.

"I love what you've done with the place," he said.

"You should," Lena Dunham cut in. "You paid for it."

Coates shook his head and glowered. "You people with your HBO money."

Gregory placed an arm over Frank's shoulder.

"I'm going to borrow Frank for a moment. Miguel, why don't you show Helene the new painting? You won't believe it, Helene. It's a Leonora Carrington!"

Then Gregory led Frank to a room in what used to be the adjoining townhouse, where Cormac McCarthy stood holding a pool cue and levelling a pitiless gaze at a scattering of snooker balls.

The next half hour might have been half a year. McCarthy congratulated Frank on the extension of the HBO deal.

"You know about television?"

McCarthy uttered a laugh as dry as the West Texas plain.

"Ah, yes," Frank said. "It was a joke… because you are… timeless and uh, you know."

McCarthy set up the balls and let Frank break and when it was his turn, the older man stalked the table like some inexorable presence, sinking balls and running up his score. Frank, increasingly beset by vertigo, felt relieved to make it through the game without damaging the felt.

As Frank struggled to make post-game conversation, a chorus of voices reached him: "Fairytale! Fairytale!"

McCarthy smiled at him and gestured in the direction of the sound.

"I think that's your cue. Don't want to leave your fans waiting."

McCarthy led Frank to the front room, where space had been cleared in front of a white baby grand piano.

"They say this is some kind of tradition at Gregory's Christmas parties."

Frank felt the eyes of the room upon him and came to the realization that he was expected to entertain. If only he hadn't abandoned piano lessons when he was sixteen and afraid of looking gay, uncool or both.

"Fairytale! Fairytale!"

The crowd was relentless. Was that a push in the back? He stepped forward and slid into place at the bench, closing his eyes and concentrating and trying to recall the placement of middle C. As his fingers landed on the keys, they began to move as if of their own volition and tease out the intro to *Fairytale of New York* and before Frank could stop himself, he began to sing of spending Christmas Eve in the drunk tank. He *had* done this before.

When the tempo changed after the first two stanzas, Miguel stepped forward and, in a valiant attempt at a stage-Irish accent, launched into the Kirsty MacColl part, singing the lines of the narrator's long-lost love. The crowd cheered as he and Miguel sang their duet and those cheers came to a crescendo when they built toward the song's drunken argument. Toasts were made, voices called for an encore and Miguel leaned in and kissed Frank on the cheek and whispered in his ear: "We need to talk. Guest bedroom in five minutes."

It took all that time for Frank to extricate himself from the crowd and reach the top floor of the southern townhouse. Miguel closed the door behind Frank and gestured for him to sit on an antique-looking, pressed-back chair in front of a dressing table. In one hand, Miguel held a bound manuscript.

"What's going on?" Frank asked. "What's that?"

Miguel placed the manuscript on the table, face down.

"Tell me what you know about me."

Frank gazed at Miguel, looking for clues.

"You're Gregory's partner? You're originally from Mexico?"

Miguel nodded.

Frank started to search his memory, then stopped. Instead, he began to speak without consciously willing the words, like an actor who has rehearsed his lines so well he can discover them in the moment.

"You're a physicist. You teach at Berkeley. You made full professor last year and Gregory held a big dinner to celebrate. And it wasn't just the promotion. You published an important paper. Gregory called you a future Nobel Prize winner."

"Interesting. Now tell me about your rain pain."

Rain pain again?

"Helene mentioned that today. It sounds as if I should remember but... does it have something to do with the scar on my ass?"

"Peru."

Frank repeated the word and it came to him in a flood. "Peru. During the Sendero Luminoso years. I was working with Médecins Sans Frontières on an immunization drive in the Andes near Ayacucho. I was running back to the truck to get more vaccines when they attacked. They sprayed rifle fire and tossed grenades and the next thing I remember I was face down in the street and it felt as if my leg was on fire."

Miguel pointed at the manuscript. "Gregory says the chapter on Peru is the high point of your memoir. They're thinking Ryan Gosling for the movie version."

Frank turned it over and read the title: *What You Know*, by Frank Milovic. It was the story of how he came to be who he was today, whoever that was. He turned and examined himself in the mirror, wondering how it was that the face seemed at once familiar and alien.

"Do you know what's happening to me?"

Miguel leaned over Frank and joined him in scrutinizing the reflection.

"Have you ever felt that there was a moment in your life that was a hinge? A time when you made a decision that changed everything? And perhaps ever since then, you have thought about the life you might have had if you had chosen otherwise?"

Frank's eyes widened in recognition. There was such a moment. He recalled speaking, as a high school student, to a visiting writer-in-residence after a public lecture at the University of Alberta. He had said to the distinguished novelist that he wanted to be a writer. And he had asked the man's opinion of his plan to attend journalism school.

"Do you want to be a reporter?"

"Well, I really want to write novels, but—"

"Then write novels."

"But I need to do something to make a living."

The distinguished visiting writer made a dismissive gesture.

"You need to make a living. But to be a writer you need to live. Get a job that gets you out in the world doing something. A reporter watches. You need to do. Chekhov was a doctor. Conrad was a seaman. Orwell was an imperial policeman."

Then the distinguished visiting writer turned away and began signing copies of his latest novel.

For decades, Frank had replayed that conversation and imagined the life he'd have led if he'd taken that advice. What if, instead of going to journalism school, he'd taken that paramedic course at Grant MacEwan College and maybe joined the Army Reserve as a medic? What if he'd learned how to operate heavy equipment and stockpiled cash by driving bulldozers in the oilsands, then taken off to explore South America and study Spanish, maybe stopping off in the Atacama Desert or the Amazon Basin to work for some Australian-owned mining company or serve as a fixer on an anthropological expedition? What if he'd taken all that experience and gone to work for Médecins Sans Frontières during the Sendero Luminoso war?

Jesus, he'd have had a hell of a story to tell. A story like that would have kindled a fire in him to write, a lot more than working as a reporter ever did. Maybe he'd have even kept up the piano playing, written some world-weary Warren Zevon-style ballads.

"What was your big physics paper about?" Frank already knew.

"Possible worlds."

Frank quoted something from memory. "The universe is consciousness. You wrote that."

"*Claro.*"

Frank realized with Miguel's "*Claro*" that the entire conversation had been carried out in Spanish.

"I think you've already explained it to me, but I can't quite remember."

Miguel began to pace the room, looking every bit the professor. "There is a universe in which a young Miguel Paredes Guzman decides not to continue in graduate school. He worries that it will be difficult to find a university position in theoretical physics. The fellowship he has been offered to the Max Planck Institute will require two cold, wet winters in Germany. His mother and his father, after spending so much money to send him to California for his undergraduate degree, urge him to take the job that has been offered at a rapidly growing technology company that allows people to share holiday photos and news articles. So he does, and he makes a good living, but he always wonders if he might have discovered something important, something fundamental, about the working of the universe."

"And he does?"

"In a manner of speaking. One of the Miguels does. The Miguel who has fallen in love with a handsome, wealthy literary agent discovers that focused consciousness causes the alternative world to come into existence. How does he make this discovery? It all starts with a question. What was the universe before the Big Bang? It must have been nothing, but a nothing with the potential to be something. And so Miguel—I—focus on what creates this potential. And it turns out the answer is 'thinking.'

As philosophers have suggested for centuries: 'I think, therefore I am,' 'in the beginning was the Word.' The Big Bang happened because the people in the potential universe that it would create were thinking about it."

"That's impossible."

"And that is why I will win the Nobel Prize. Anybody can prove the obvious. It takes a genius to prove the impossible. So then, if conscious thought created the one universe in which we all started out, can conscious thought create a series of other universes? Universes that might exist if people had made different choices, taken bigger risks, or even continued to go to their piano lessons?"

Frank pictured a version of himself sitting at a desk in the *Edmonton Journal* newsroom and fantasizing about a more exciting life. It's a dreary Edmonton November on a Wednesday and he's writing headlines and cutlines for a page of stories on a new suburban development in Sherwood Park and his mind wanders to other places, other times in the life of another Frank Milovic.

"So I caused this universe to exist, just by thinking about it?"

"Yes. One of the Miguels worked out the math. It is very complicated."

"Which Miguel are you?"

"Which Frank are you?"

Frank thought about it for a moment. He remembered getting hired at the *Journal* after two years at the *Red Deer Advocate*. He remembered eating green onion cakes at the Edmonton Fringe, long weekend camping trips in Jasper, years of hoping that maybe this would be the winter when the Oilers would finally get back on track. He also remembered Army boot camp and scraping away frozen muskeg with the blade of a forty-nine-ton Cat D9. It was all swirling through his brain. And now he recalled returning from Peru and beginning his first novel and meeting Helene and celebrating with her when he sold his first book and every book that followed. And he remembered moving to California when Hollywood came sniffing around, and he remembered meeting producers from HBO, and buying the chalet in Jackson with the money from the second season.

"I don't really know."

"I think you're both. As am I. As is, perhaps, Gregory."

"Gregory?"

"Don't you think his client list is rather improbably comprehensive?"

Frank reached for the manuscript of his memoir. He began to flip through it, memories jumping off the pages.

"Okay. Say you're right. This is my fantasy universe. What are you doing in it?"

"I thought that this universe was mine alone, but I feel that these worlds are collapsing into one another now. Picture a skyscraper, billions of storeys high. The floors and ceilings are made of something hard but erodible, let us say sandstone. One day a man succeeds in boring a hole through his floor. It is a very large building and a very small hole, so it shouldn't threaten the structure's integrity. But sandstone is composed of tiny grains glued together by great pressure. In time, that little hole becomes larger and this person falls through the hole and perhaps the people around him do as well."

Frank tried to visualize the original floor plan of Miguel's billion-storey skyscraper. He drew a mental map of the world of what he already thought of as Frank 1.0. He drove a Hyundai. He lived in a 1960s bungalow in St. Albert. He wrote about housing developments most of the time, because real estate ads were one of the few things keeping the newspaper business afloat these days, but the highlight of his work week was the one day he spent editing or writing reviews for the steadily shrinking book section. He'd even reviewed McCarthy's last two books himself.

Miguel reached forward and closed the copy of Frank's memoir. "We should return to the party and I should put this back in Gregory's office."

"Give me a minute."

Miguel patted Frank on the shoulder. "They loved our song."

"They always do," said Frank. "*Verdad*?"

Frank watched Miguel depart and stood to look out the window on a San Francisco winter night. It had begun to rain. His buttock and thigh hurt, as they always did in the rain, ever since Peru. Time for Tylenol and a bag of frozen peas. He tried a couple of stretches Helene had showed him.

Helene, he felt certain, existed in both worlds. In one, Frank remained in Edmonton and went to see an attractive, young, recently divorced physiotherapist after throwing out his back by skiing the full 55-km Birkebeiner at Cooking Lake. After his back was better, surprised by his own boldness, he called her up to ask her out. In the other world, he returned to Edmonton with his shrapnel injury and had a series of appointments with the same physiotherapist. So maybe they were meant to be together, in any universe. It was a romantic thought.

Frank closed the door quietly and sought to return to the party unobserved. As he crept down the stairs, he heard Helene's voice and something about the tone of it made him stop and listen while out of sight.

"I know it sounds ungrateful, but I wish so often that Frank didn't have this kind of success. Is that terrible of me? You know, my first husband and I had property in the bush up near Redwater. Just enough for a little hobby farm. I could have gotten a loan and bought him out, but instead we just sold it and split the money. I've regretted that for years. If I could live in the country and raise chickens and goats and plant a big garden, that would be the life I'd love."

"It is not terrible," Miguel said. "It is only human to think of the life you do not live."

Things were winding down and the guests were dispersing when Frank rejoined Helene, and when he noticed the sadness in her eyes that lingered despite the Botox she swore, prior to California, she would never get. He leaned toward her and kissed her and asked if she would like to go home.

"I can drive," he said. "I never even saw Gregory's wine cellar."

She laughed, a short laugh, not without humour and not without a trace of bitterness.

"Sure," she said. "We'd better run. The goats are going to need feeding."

Goats?

LURKERS IN THE LEAVES

Chadwick Ginther

The night I met Emily Locke was the first time my head was cut off.

Emily wasn't her name. Not really. Just a designation given to a dream.

I've seen her every night since.

In dreams.

Nightmares.

Her skin was wooden, but not like the bark of a tree. It looked smooth—sanded. Leaves, lush with all the green of spring, cascaded over her shoulders like ringlets. She was the kind of person who never let a single thought go unspoken. If I believed in faeries, I'd say she was one. Tall and willowy, whoever—whatever—she was, she was not of this earth.

They say if you die in a dream, you'll die in your bed, too.

I don't know about that.

There was nothing but death waiting for me in the long reach of night, and I'm still here.

I went with her into the woods that first time, thinking I'd get lucky, even if I was too young to know exactly what lucky meant. I just knew the way she made me feel—confused, aroused; terrified and brave, all at once, like a great jumble of leaves, waiting to be tumbled into.

She gave me something—a scarf, maybe—and bound the token around my waist and it felt good to have her arms encircle me. Her breasts brushed my chest as she tied the knot.

That felt good, too.

Emily pulled me down into the leaves and we rolled, kissing. My nostrils were filled with the heavy, earthy scents of fall, even though I knew back home on the farm, it was summer. She had me on my back, straddling me, and reached behind her. I thought she was going to take her shirt off. I stiffened, anticipating.

This time. This time.

Somewhere distant, I felt a sense of urgency. There were whispers, carried on a cold breeze, from just beyond my sight.

Nononono.

Something hard poked at my back. We'd disturbed the leaves and I saw them: bones. A great midden full of them, bleached pale white and shining like silver under the glow of the moon. Emily wasn't undressing. She had her axe.

Again.

As it descended, I put my arms up knowing—always knowing—I was too late. There was only heat, and iron, and the taste of pennies. My head tumbled from my shoulders, and watched, unblinking, as my body ran.

It stood up and ran.

I thought idly of runaway chickens on my parents' farm. Wind bent the young branches and the leaves gathered over my head and eyes, mercifully blinding me. I became dizzy, wanting to throw up, but my mouth wasn't connected to my stomach and only a hollow, dry gasp escaped.

Whispers filled my ears. I heard them, but I refused to listen. I tried to scream. All that passed my lips was a wheeze. My body tripped, its foot caught in a tree root. I fell. And they were on me.

That's it.

I'm done.

This is all.

But it wasn't.

It never is.

○

I grew up on a farm, but when I left for university, I fell in love with the city.

Its noise.

Its stink.

The closeness.

It had its share of trees, even a small forest within its perimeter, but many seemed sick. Tired. Disease had muted their voices, making them easier to ignore.

There was a vastness to the city's claustrophobia, as steel and concrete replaced fields and bluffs, dwarfing the expanse of nothing that had always filled my vision. I hadn't been back to the farm since Christmas. I hadn't yet broken it to my parents I wasn't going back. Every time I turned around, I discovered something new: new friends, new foods; new pleasures, new stories. Something that could never have been in my old home. Until I discovered something old: *Emily Locke.*

A young sidewalk tree hissed her name amid the wind. The tree was a spindly, babbling thing. I meant to ignore it, gulping the beer I'd been nursing to mute its excited voice. But then I saw her.

I was at a café in the city's Little Italy district. This Emily didn't have leafy ringlets, or shaped and sanded skin. She had black, black hair, eyes the colour of acorns, and tanned skin. A gust of wind caught enough of her shirt that I could see the sharply defined white line that had never seen the sun.

She caught me staring. I looked away, embarrassed, and went back to scribbling in my notebook. Seeing her brought back my dreams—and nightmares—confusion and arousal, I was terrified and brave. Looking up, I saw *her* now staring at *me*. I snapped my notebook shut, stood up and walked over to introduce myself.

She spoke first, after tapping her lips with her index finger. "Let me guess, Jack. Jack Green."

"Close," I said, wondering at the coincidence. Jack was my middle name. "But it's George, not Jack. Greene with an 'e', as in Graham Greene." She cocked her head at me and I worried I was being pretentious, but it always got misspelled, and the pre-emptive correction was habit now, as much as affectation. "The writer, not the colour."

"Is it now?" she answered. "Sally Black, no 'e.'" We both smiled. The further coincidence of our last names being colours was enough to continue the conversation, and we talked and laughed. Hit it off. She didn't cut off my head.

This time.

We went on a date. Then another. I still had my head. She still called me Jack, but I liked the hint of tease in her voice when she did so.

A third date. That changed things for me—for both of us. We knew what that convention meant. Expectation sat heavily between us. I was nervous, but for once no dread stained that sensation. It wouldn't be my first time, but it *had* been a while, and I wasn't nearly as experienced as I'd told my dormmates. We were out for a walk near one of the city's riverside parks, and I spent as much energy trying to block the whispering trees as I did trying not to say something stupid. It was a cool night, winter still biting at spring, and her breath hot in my ear, she whispered, "I know a place."

She tugged me toward the park. I trembled as she clambered over the fence. I didn't want to go in, but I wanted to be anywhere she was. Especially where we could be alone, in the dark. I navigated the fence with as much dignity as I could muster. She led me toward the river; I could hear its fat gurgle, groaning at the banks. I followed her down a set of wooden stairs that seemed vaguely familiar, although I had never been to this part of Winnipeg before.

I stumbled down a couple more steps, dragged along by Sally's insistent tug. I looked over my shoulder, and saw Parliament and the Peace Tower rising up against a blue sky. But those were in Ottawa…

A blink and the leaves had buried the blue sky; it was night again. Night still. *Weird.*

The trees whispered, "Remember."

This couldn't be happening. *Not now.* I had a flask in my pocket. Just in case. My fingers trembled. My arms shook. Sally jerked me along and the flask fell from my hand, clattering away into darkness. I shut them out, but they were still there. Waiting. Lurking.

I didn't want to listen to the damned trees, but I couldn't help but remember. As a child I'd visited Ottawa with my parents. I'd fallen down some wooden steps, much like these, trying to get a look at a damned cat. There should be two hundred and sixty wooden steps leading down to the base of the Rideau River. My sister had counted them—she'd been so proud, it had been the highest number she'd counted to.

Sally's eyes narrowed, watching me over her shoulder. She ran, ever downward, heedless as she stared, and didn't once slow her manic descent. She scooped up my flask from where it had landed. "Missing something?"

I took it from her, and opened it one handed. I drank. Whiskey slid past my lips, and dribbled over my chin as she jerked me away.

"Was that supposed to be for you, or for me?" Sally asked. She kissed me then, as if not wanting to waste a drop of whiskey. I hoped I had enough.

I watched every step as I followed Sally, worrying at each before I put my full weight upon it, counting as I went, estimating how many steps I'd already taken, each number whispered as I touched the wood. Two hundred. My breath caught. I hit the magic number. Two hundred and sixty. The steps continued down, but at this point there was a tree that had never given shade to Ottawa.

The Halfway Tree, a towering willow that rose along the Trans-Canada Highway used by Manitoba travellers to mark time between the cities of Brandon and Winnipeg. It'd survived the expansion of the highway, truck collisions and lightning strikes. But I was pretty sure it'd never moved.

"Help," it begged.

I'm not listening to you.

Scraggly sticks poked out from its scarred trunk.

"C'mon," Sally said. "You're not ready for that."

"Ready for what?"

I rounded the trunk, my fingers drifting lazily over the bark. The alcohol burned in my belly. It wasn't enough to quiet the trees. I should be able to see a paved walkway and a bicycle path along the Rideau right now. I should be flailing in the Red River in Winnipeg. And at the same time, I should be twenty kilometres outside of Portage La Prairie.

My heart pounded. Sweat gathered in the small of my back. My brain swam in too many currents, and I didn't know which would save me, or drown me. A glance up the stairs. I'd come so far. Sally smiled, beckoning. Where to go? Deeper down, where dreams and nightmares waited, or up?

There is something about that path not travelled.

The road not taken.

It'd take more courage than could be found in my flask. I lifted a foot, took a deep breath, and as I did in every dream, every nightmare, I followed, swimming into the green. Crickets and grasshoppers joined in song with the drone of cicadas. Songbirds, familiar and strange, harmonized.

It felt as if I was in *every* forest, all in one. There were redwoods next to mangroves, oaks mingled with baobabs, jack pines and palms. It shouldn't be. None of it.

I followed Sally and I recognized trees, like old friends leaping from a crowd of strangers. Trees I'd climbed as a boy, missing their ramshackle playhouses and rope ladders, but still I knew them. Another had been struck by lightning long before I was born, before my mother was born, and toppled over on its side, but it still lived, and every child chose that tree first to clamber upon, monkey-like.

My first kiss was under that dogwood—I'd carved my initials in that one, along with those of my first lover. She's married now. It rested next to the little babbler from Corydon, where I'd met Sally.

Not all of the trees were friends.

I've never trusted them at the best of times. Blame my nightmares if you must. The whisper of the wind through their leaves. Waiting through the winter, seemingly dead, but living still. A sound startled me, and I spun, looking for its origin, and there it was: the young cottonwood that had *tap tap tapped* on my window all winter, chilling me colder than any drafty farmhouse. I saw the tree that broke my nose when I was running and tripped over a root. Knobby bark blossomed and bloomed like tumorous growths all over its trunk. That's the image I saw when I thought of cancer—and the day mom told me grandma wasn't coming out of the hospital.

There was the Hanging Tree, talked about in hushed whispers by schoolchildren, with its branch where the bark had been rubbed raw—probably from a tire swing. But the tree lived in a courthouse yard and everyone had been convinced that scar was the result of a noose. Even as an adult, I shuddered as I walked under that limb. The Hanging Tree's voice was the sound of a rope burn, twined fibers ripping skin. *Swing with me.*

I reared back against Sally's insistent tug. She looked pissed. Scared. Both. "George—"

"They're here," I said, not knowing of whom I spoke, but *knowing* all the same.

"I know."

"They… want…" I didn't know what. I couldn't hear that—or didn't want to.

"I know that, too."

The sounds of the green surrounded me. The light clatter of branches. The whistle of leaves. A chittering squirrel. A raven's *quork*. A jaguar's scream.

I shouldn't be here, where my nightmares were real. My heart pounded. The barking exhales of my breath were all I could hear. There were things in the woods. Ancient grudges. Remembrance of a time before humanity. Things wanting that time to return.

My parents told me my dreams were only my imagination. That I was hearing things. Seeing things. I was. I *did* hear them. I *did* see them.

Things.

I stopped talking about the dreams so Mom and Dad wouldn't worry—or judge. Just my imagination. Not something I have a dearth of. But that's how they get you. The things waiting in the trees. The lurkers. In the black of nightmares, they plant their seeds to grow and choke out your life.

I slowed my steps, and for the first time, I didn't feel the drag of Sally pulling me ever downward. We'd stopped, and she brushed her hand through my hair.

"You've come this far for me, my Jack of the Green," she said. "How far will you go for yourself?"

I took her hand—it felt sticky, like sap—and looked up the stairs. "Can I go back?"

She smiled. "I don't know. *Can you?*"

Every important moment or event in my life, I'd look up and see a tree observing. I tied a line, the weft and warp of my life, from root to leaf, from this evening, to my very first memory. They're scattered in parks and on streets in all different towns and cities and countries—they are everywhere I've ever been, and all here together. I closed my eyes. They're all here. I *felt* them. Waiting for me. Whispering in a language older than time.

I'd tried drinking, it was the thing writers did, wasn't it? Sleeping pills weren't enough. They caused me to dream deeper, more vividly, and to be lost in a drowning sensation, unable to escape. Alcohol, at least—especially a good blackout drunk—held them at bay. For a while, until my grades slipped. I knew if I continued down that path, it would terminate with me home on the farm. The last place I wanted to ride out my days. Until I thought of returning to the trees and the clearing. The trees of the farm waited, wind breaks surrounding the yard. Here they stood stark against a verdant green, like a fence, winter bare and overgrown, as if they hadn't been pruned since my childhood.

"You can still go home," Sally said.

Thinking of those trees, I *knew* Sally had secrets she wasn't sharing, I couldn't. I needed to know who—what—I was. We pushed through the bush, bare branches scraping our skin. I held on to Sally's warm touch, my insistence now dragged her forward. Counting the stairs long forgotten. When I finally left the steps, the air swelled with life. Richer, somehow, than what I was used to breathing.

There was no car exhaust. No chemical stink from pesticides. The air tasted green and my body prickled with gooseflesh. Pollen twinkled in starlight. The olfactory and aural stimuli taking me back to the dreams; the terror and desire that mingled together when I thought of Emily Locke. The same admixture I felt now, watching Sally Black kick off her sandals and twirl, delightedly, amid the tall grasses.

"Home again, home again," she sang. "It's been altogether too long, and not nearly long enough."

I knew the feeling. I felt the same whenever I visited family.

She clasped my hands, and spun me 'round and 'round, toward the centre of the clearing and the great, gnarled oak tree at its centre. A brown, leafy blanket and a peppering of acorns obscured the grass beneath the oak's span, though the tree itself was in full green. Stairs ringed the clearing like the spokes of a wheel. They felt packed tight as peas, but I could feel the gulf of miles and oceans between them. Another woman led another man into the clearing.

Spin.

A man leading a woman.

Spin.

Another man. Another woman.

Spin.

Two men.

Spin.

Two women.

Spin.

The trees whipped past, and I felt like a child riding a carousel, watching the crowd for the safety of my parents, season after season blurred, one into the next. The clearing filled with all manner of people locked in twirling embraces of their own. I was filled in turn with hope, pride, resignation and fear. New buds became the full green of summer; brown, red, and gold scattered, leaving bare branches, dusted with snow. In those winter forests, the *tap tap tapping* of a dogwood on a frost-crusted windowpane grew closer, twinned with the whispers of my youth: malevolent and bent, twisted and mean.

Those dead winter branches *moved*. And it wasn't from the wind.

Leaves rustled and rose before that great oak, spinning, as if caught in a gale. In the moonlight, the bark of the old tree formed a man's face. I knew that face. From carvings in old buildings and churches; from New Age stores. Knobs of rounded bark where branches had been cut, or broken in ages past formed eyes and a nose; a yawning hollow in its trunk formed the mouth. The wind originated from that hollow, gusting wheezing breaths. Roots tangled like limbs, sunk into the earth, a tired old man, this Green Man, crouching at his labours, but too diligent to give them up.

In one voice, Sally, and those who, like her, had led lovers down strange stairs, said, "Welcome, Jack of the Green."

Was that why she'd called me Jack? What did it mean?

Drifting leaves tumbled, criss-crossing each other's paths, following no wind. They swirled about me, brittle edges slicing, drawing thin roads of blood.

Seed. Fear. Sun. Food.

I heard the rumbling burr of the oak, in every cut of a leaf.

Who will whisper the green words to you, Green George?

Sally asked, breath hot on my neck, "Will you answer?"

Will you be a champion for growing things when they face the Long White?

I didn't know what the Green Man meant. The call and answer smacked of ritual, and reminded me of church—and a faith I'd feigned, but never felt. Until now. "How?"

"Will you be a tempter?" Sally said with a smile.

A warrior? The Green Man rumbled.

"A hunter?"

From beyond the clearing, the click-clack voices of sticks on glass, and branches breaking said, *Will you be food?*

Another chorus, *Even trees hunger.*

Anger filled me at what was being asked of me. Of what had been done *to* me.

"You have chosen," Sally said. She seemed pleased.

No.

The roots pulsed, stretching, cracking; spraying earth and reaching for us.

Even trees must feed.

No.

The word didn't come, but Sally still heard, and answered, "Yes, George. It's time."

Sally pushed me into a pile of leaves. Something hard cracked against my back. I knew it wasn't a tree root. I knew what lurked under those leaves. That rounded thing prodding my back was a skull. Would my bones moulder here, making a bed for Sally's next victim?

She leaned forward, *shushing* me as I strained against her grip. Her skin had taken on the same wooden appearance it had in my dreams, but felt neither smooth, nor sanded. Instead it was rough, hard, like the bark of a tree. Leaves, drained by the inevitability of autumn, dropped over her shoulders. Her green scarf became a twisted lattice of ivy and briar thorns.

Sally pinned my hands and I felt her fingers stretch, growing, rooting us to the ground. Dragging my arms into the earth. Her scarf crept, alive, winding around my waist. Thorns dug in. Blood streamed down my legs. I *hoped* it was blood.

"I'm tired," Sally said. "But I could stay here forever. I *want* to stay here forever."

"I don't." I choked the words out, trying not to make them a whimper. Didn't succeed. I knew, *knew,* that axe was coming. "I want to be anywhere but here. I want to be *every*where but here."

She canted her head and her acorn eyes regarded me, curiously. "Too late."

Her eyes rolled free, acorns in truth, and popped into my gaping mouth. I fought not to swallow them, slipping them under my tongue. In the black hollow of her sockets, I could see every year she'd lived, every spring, every harvest, and every winter. There were hundreds. She'd seen the birth of manned flight, had lived through more wars than I had years. I saw her leading me down into this place of dream and nightmare. I saw every other man and woman who'd followed her for another glimpse of those acorn brown eyes.

"Plant me somewhere you love," she said. "And visit when you can."

Her voice husky, with what? Sadness? Golden sap trickled

from where her eyes had been. I knew why she'd chosen me, followed me through dreams, nightmares, the waking world—and finally, here. I knew why she'd given me her scarf, that green token. I knew what the whispers had said to me that first night, I knew what I'd refused to hear. What I wasn't ready to hear.

What I'd spent my entire life fleeing.

I knew them now, the night whisperers. The lurkers in the leaves.

The fallen.

The discards.

The ones who'd made it this far and wouldn't commit to the Green. Snapped and broken, the twig men came out of winter, bodies cracking with cold. They came from places that had once held lush forests, now—forever—trapped and crushed by ice. But they remembered. And hungered. And if given their way, they would see everywhere succumb. As they had.

A Long White, without end.

They moved jerkily, legs and arms different lengths. Vines and scarves, not unlike the token that Sally had given me, bound their branches together, like muscles over wooden skeletons. They bore axes, like Sally had in my dreams, but rusted as if they'd spent a winter in the snow. Bramble-haired, with thorns for teeth, they wore jackets of mismatched leather. Hints of eyes and noses told me that the leather had never come from a cow.

An axe flashed, but not for me. Sally's head came free from her shoulders, falling to the leaves. Green turned red, and then brown. Finally, crumbling like a dry leaf crushed in a fist, Sally blew away. The last of the ivy tightened over me. In our last moment of joining, I knew why me.

I was free.

But still trapped.

One of the lurkers loomed over me, seeming tall as a glacier-covered mountain. We fought. The other supplicants, sacrifices, whatever you'd wish to call us, they fought, too. The buried bones felt like they were holding my hands as I struggled to free my arms from the earth. To do what? Try and block an axe?

The axe fell.

Heat.

Iron.

The taste of pennies.

No vertigo this time. I'd experienced the sensation for so long, in so many dreams, I'd long become inured to the shock of having my head taken off. I was more shocked I *wasn't* shocked.

The lurker reached down and his gnarled hands tugged at my belt. Thorns dug into my flesh and blood oozed past the barbs. The lurker turned away from me with a creaking groan to find another to murder. He knew I'd be back, and he could be patient for his chance.

In my dreams, my body ran.

I had always run.

Not this time.

My head closed its eyes. It seemed easier, somehow, not to look. My arms jerked free of the midden. The grasp of bones having no more hold, I stood. Old flesh and bones had turned to dirt and trickled through my fingers.

Walking forward with determined steps, each like pulling up a rooted tree, I lifted my head from the leaves and set it upon my shoulders. The creeping ivy grew up my torso, infiltrating my flesh, and I felt every jab as the reaching vines sutured me together. I took a breath. It felt like my first; a hollow gasp. Fingers tightened reflexively, eyes blinked and watered.

The lurkers advanced. Tearing tokens free of bodies where they could, fighting to make fresh bodies where they could not. I knew they wanted to burrow into that great oak and destroy it. But I also knew they couldn't—not while we held the tokens. While *we* lived, the Green Man lived. He might be too tired to pull up his roots and fight them himself, but he had his Jacks and his Sallys and within us was the potential for his renewal. But only if we could leave this place and get to our home. I'd lost track of where home was. But the set of stairs by which I left didn't matter. Only that I left.

I rushed for stairs—any stairs. As the lurkers clawed at me, I thought of the resilience of the Halfway Tree, the Monkey Tree, and my skin hardened, as if I wore thick bark armour. The lurkers' fingers scrabbled and snapped against me.

The other survivors scrambled for stairs and their exit, too. Not all of us made it. Some were dragged deep into the lurkers' cold woods. With each of us that fell, I saw the Green Man's branches droop; leaves wilting and falling.

So long as any of us escaped—so long as *one* of us was left to fight, and strive, and grow, the Long White would stay at bay. The Green Man would keep whispering green words and green dreams to fools like me.

I pounded up the stairs. I didn't recognize the sky above. The stars were different. Trees too. But I knew their names, both what science called them and what they called themselves. I ran up those stairs for a seeming eternity. Night sky became day. The sun warmed me and I stretched up to greet it. I could feel it nourish me. Washing away the blood, and fear, and trials.

I spat out Sally's acorn eyes, and wondered where I should plant her. And what we'd talk about when she grew. A tree broke through the ties of a rail line that cut through a residential neighbourhood. I wasn't home. But I was. The whole of the world was my home now. A break of grass on either side of the rails. I kneeled and touched the fragile leaf. The first thing I saw upon my escape. Another memory, another moment tied to the green. I heard its infant whisper.

And I listened.

YET ANOTHER ROADSIDE MANIFESTATION

Wayne Santos

The last time Reyna Macatangay was in rural Alberta, she had neither a college degree nor access to magical energy or alien relics. She hoped the stark upgrade in the circumstances of her life would make this visit a better one, but that was probably wishful thinking.

"I'm a professional," she said to no one in particular, experiencing one of those rare moments when she wished she still smoked. "And I have a job to do."

It was early in Vegreville. Too early. The night was about to give way to dawn, and in the distance, in the middle of the Elks/Kinsmen Park, stood the thing. The egg. The Vegreville Pysanka, they called it.

Even though it had been built in 1973, it looked like a Playstation 2 fever dream. A giant Easter egg, composed of nothing but anodized aluminum triangles, sitting under a dark sky.

It was the second-largest of its kind in the world, but according to Reyna's sources, what made it really impressive was the damn thing was about to hatch.

And still, the help she had been told to expect had not shown up.

She couldn't really blame the late arrival, whoever they were. Being told to show up at dawn at the site of a giant Easter egg and then "stand by for further instructions" was never going to go over very well. Especially with law enforcement.

"I'm a professional," she said again, watching her breath escape from her mouth with a white, vaporous crispness that again reminded her of cigarettes she no longer smoked. She really wished now that the cops, or other duly designated representatives, would hurry the fuck up and get here already, so at least she could complain to a person and not just the air.

The eastern sky was lightening when she heard the distant sound of an engine.

The RCMP logo and sirens mounted on the top of the car left no doubt as to who had arrived.

Reyna pulled up the collar on her coat and huddled inside it in a vain attempt to keep warm. Mornings in Alberta. She'd forgotten how cold they could be at this time of year.

The car pulled up and someone got out of it, trudging cautiously towards Reyna. It took a few moments for Reyna to make out the details, the blond hair tied back, probably in braids, the slim face, the tired, worn, but feminine gait. She carried a flashlight, the kind that could stun a cow if swung with enough force, but it wasn't on.

"Do Mounties smoke?"

"I'm a peace officer. And not on duty." She patted a pocket in her coat. "I only taste the adventure when I have the time and required metre clearance from the nearest building." She turned the flashlight on and evaluated Reyna. "Are you the reason I'm here?"

"I'm further instructions, if that's what you mean. Although usually I'm filed as Reyna Macatangay."

"Officer Senko," the woman said. "Macatangay, that's..."

"Filipino."

"I thought Filipino was all Sanchez and Mendoza and stuff."

"My ancestors were playing hooky the day the Spanish were taking our names away and handing out new ones."

"Fair enough," Officer Senko said. "So, are you going to tell me why we got a call in at the Vegreville detachment telling us we needed to send someone with legal authority down here before 7 a.m.?"

"Are you local, Officer Senko? Like, did you grow up here?"

"Is that your roundabout way of asking if I'm a hick?"

Reyna bit her lip and felt herself shrinking. This was a cop. In Alberta. And coming back to the Prairies had an unnerving effect on her that she experienced nowhere else. It was a cinematic overlap, a twining and superimposition of herself now. A self-made woman, one who had proven herself to the people that counted, who had a reputation for getting results. That was paired with the uncertain girl she remembered being here, the one who stood out in a sea of white students, who eventually stopped bringing homemade lunches from school because the smell brought down the wrath of the white kids who had zero tolerance for "stinky gook food" in a sea of peanut butter sandwiches and drink boxes of chocolate milk or apple juice.

"Professional," Reyna whispered under her breath. She wasn't a little brown girl with no power or authority talking to the big, scary police. She could hold her own against a badge. She'd done it before, just never here.

"What?"

She closed her eyes and opened them slowly. "I wasn't implying anything. I was just wondering what you knew about the—Pysanka."

"You know it's called that?"

Reyna nodded and hitched a thumb due west. "Used to be an Edmonton girl. Not my first time here."

"I trained in Edmonton," Officer Senko said. "Used to be?"

"Moved because of work. I live deep in enemy territory now." Reyna was never sure what it was about growing up here that made phrases like that equate to "Ontario," but it was still something she shared in common with anyone that grew up here.

Senko looked her up and down. "Must be some work if you can drop orders on law enforcement." She regarded the egg. "Anyway, yeah, local girl. That thing's been there as long as I can remember. Kind of a twofer. Supposed to be giving props to all the Ukrainians that settled this area, but it's for the RCMP too, that was the only way the town was going to get the Fed money for it."

"Did you know the guy that helped design this thing was an aeronautical engineer?" Reyna asked.

"Nope. Does it matter?"

"That depends. The precis I got on the guy who came up with this was less complete than I'd like, but it confirmed one bad thing about this situation."

"And that is?"

"He cut a deal with… unauthorized forces, and that"—she pointed towards the egg—"is the result of the supranatural deal."

"The wha—you mean supernatural?"

"I don't know if it's that yet. That's something mystical, maybe chaotic or irrational in nature. This could just as easily be something extraterrestrial, or from another timeline, in which case it's just beyond what we understand of our world, but not magic. Supranatural, until proven otherwise."

Officer Senko stared hard. "The phone call said I was here on official business, but they didn't tell me the business was conducting a sobriety test and bringing someone in. One second, I left the PAS in the back." She turned and made her way to her car.

"If you're going back in there, then maybe just put on the seatbelt and stay there," Reyna suggested. "Maybe keep your hand near the ignition and be ready to split if things get bad."

Officer Senko stopped and turned again. "What is that, some kind of drunk threat?"

Ah. Skepticism and thinly veiled hostility. Reyna was starting to feel on familiar ground now. This, at least, she knew how to handle professionally. "A safety recommendation," she said.

Officer Senko resumed her march to the car. "I'm pretty sure that breathalyzer is just in the back somewhere."

Reyna sighed and did the Model Minority thing: waiting patiently, politely and making no sudden movements.

Senko returned, adjusting the breathalyzer. "Okay, this thing is initialized."

"You're completely serious about this drunk thing?"

"Humour me."

Reyna shrugged and let Senko hold out the machine. She blew into it and watched, unsurprised, as the alcohol reading indicated zero.

"Do you want a urine sample too? I have a thermos in my car, and a few minutes to kill. Point me towards some bushes, and we've got a party."

"I'm just trying to do my job under some very weird circumstances."

"You just described my job," Reyna said. "And I'm on the clock right now, so a hundred percent sober. Just so we're all clear, there's stuff I need in this bag. I'm getting it now."

Reyna reached down to the tote bag lying on the ground and pulled out a few of her on-site kits. She chose the ones with the broadest range of results. A box with toenail clippings from an Olympian god. A crystal on a string that had been suspended for twenty years at a nexus between 6,498 different realms. A small airtight bag of unicorn shit. Dominos carved from flattened trees at the site of Tunguska. A pouch with active nanite fragments scraped off the medical console of a crashed alien spacecraft. A tiny fragment of elder god tentacle that had been confined in a Mexican jumping bean. A positronic, handheld, novelty cat calendar for the year 3941. Some duct tape.

"Are those legal?"

"The law would have to know they exist to decide whether they're legal or illegal."

"I'm still trying to make the connection between sober and... supranatural?"

Reyna nodded.

"Supranatural phenomena. That doesn't add up."

"Bell curve," Reyna said.

"What?"

"All the boring stuff is right in the middle of the bell curve. That's the median, the average, and you spend most of your life there. The supranatural stuff, just like geniuses and anime without the power of friendship, is on the extreme ends of that curve. On the margins. That's where I work, and that's where we are now."

"What?"

Reyna sighed. "Can you hold these for a sec? I need one more thing."

"What is this crap?"

"Only that little pouch is crap, the rest is all non-toxic. To most lifeforms."

Senko made a face, but Reyna pushed the things onto her and then dug through the bag. "Nullygons," she muttered to herself. "Shit, that should have been the *first* thing I dug up." She checked the sky. A thin line of dawn was spreading across the clouds like rims of rose and nostalgia. There wouldn't be much time now, her anxiousness went up a notch. She had been far too premature about the quitting smoking thing.

Reyna pulled out a pile of iridescent triangles, just nearly flat pyramids. They shimmered, even in the dim, pre-dawn light. She took back her items and handed over a pile of nullygons to Officer Senko.

Reyna put the stuff in the various pockets of her overcoat and approached the egg. It towered over her, full of quiet menace and Ukrainian pride.

"Other side," she said, motioning towards the egg. "Keep the same distance I am, and place a nullygon on the ground, make sure it's pointing towards the egg. Drop them at even intervals, you take left, I take right."

"Why are we doing this?"

"To buy some time before critical mass," Reyna said.

Senko's mouth opened. "If there's going to be an explosion."

"No, we're trying to stop something a lot worse. Now *take* these, please."

Officer Senko gasped as she placed her first nullygon on the ground, and it chimed pleasantly, like a crystal kitten waking up from a nap, stretching itself to clamp onto the ground. It shifted through a range of iridescent colours like some kind of oil spill doing its best impression of a Franziska Schenk painting.

Reyna laid her nullygons out quickly and efficiently, pleased to see Senko keeping up with her once she'd gotten over her initial shock.

Reyna checked the light again. Just in time.

The circle of nullygons was complete, and Reyna hustled them back to what she hoped was a safe distance. It probably wasn't, but it would at least give Senko some peace of mind when reality stopped working the way it was supposed to.

Reyna laid out her collection of items and artifacts on the ground at even distances from each other, a deranged knick-knack set.

Senko adjusted her hat, looking down at the alien and arcane bobs and bits. "How the hell does this even work?"

"The magical theory and the underlying alien tech principles are beyond me," she admitted. "But I know what this shit does for me. It's my Venn diagram between two or more sets of fucked-up."

"Well. That was technically English," Senko replied, not bothering to hide the utter bafflement on her face. "I guess I can add fluency in auto-complete to your list of skills."

The snipe didn't help, reminding her that here in Alberta, where she'd grown up, no one thought she was good at anything. And what she did know, and could do, no one cared about.

Then the tremor came, but it wasn't the type that anyone felt, not physically. The ground didn't shake, and there was no low rumble like thunder warming up for its big debut. This was a tremor in reality, as the accepted laws of physics shifted to accommodate some new rules.

On the ground, the nullygons glowed in shifting bands of colour and hummed. She had no idea if they could dampen something on this scale, but they were giving it their best shot.

"What the fuck..." Officer Senko whispered.

The nullygons keened shrilly, the rainbow colours shifting in speed and intensity like disco light show gone horribly awry, blobs of light and distinct patterns of sacred geometry washing across the underside of the egg. The egg itself looked blurry, but that was only because it was now vibrating.

Reyna looked at her collection of artifacts, relics, and promotional marketing. The jumping bean twitched now and again as the tiny sliver of primordial elder god resonated. The crystal from the nexus of realms rose up a few centimeters from the ground, its string making it look like a tiny helium balloon that was now glowing with sickly purple light. The same purple light that was appearing on some of the triangular pieces of anodized aluminum that made up the egg, which was producing noise of its own. Medium tones rose and fell in time to the pulsing lights of the nullygons, which were probably not going to work for much longer.

"What the hell is going on?" Officer Senko asked, probably unaware that she had sidled up closer to Reyna.

"Organism," Reyna said. "Demi-god class at least. Not from around here, not even this universe."

"You keep using English in ways that make no sense."

Some of the triangles on the egg lit up in pure white, and a single, intangible, transparent wing at least the length of a bus brushed through the shell without breaking any of it up and rose into the dawn sky. It was veined, like a batwing, but had spiky feathers at the tips.

It was joined by three more in rapid succession, all of them stretching and flexing.

The image of spectral wings rising up from a giant aluminum egg at sunrise almost made Reyna regret her distaste for social media. She stared at the ultimate '80s album cover made real, knowing it would have gotten her a million, bazillion likes if she didn't care about getting sent back to the Stone Age for breach of contract.

Beside her, Officer Senko pulled her firearm out.

"Those giant wings are rising through solid matter, do you really think a bullet is going to do anything?"

Senko uttered a sharp growl of frustration. "Well then, what else are we supposed to do? What *can* we do against that?" She waved her gun eggward like a laser pointer, which would have been about as effective.

"Narrow down our options."

"Between what, die horribly and die mysteriously?"

"I know what neighborhood I'm dealing with. Now to find the right address."

She pulled out her phone, threw up the devil horns with her right hand, waited for the biometrics to confirm it was her, then got the app up and running and handed it over to Officer Senko.

On the ground, the nullygons trembled.

"What am I supposed to do with this?" Officer Senko said as she held the phone in her hand like a grenade with its pin pulled.

"I'm going to be out of earshot for that thing." Reyna grabbed up her artifacts and stuffed them back in her tote bag, except for the ones that had reacted, they went in her pocket. She made her way towards the egg. "I need you to speak the words I shout out."

On a hunch, she reached into her bag and pulled out some wooden planks, carved with what some people might have called runes, but were actually Proto-Slavic. Some of the letters glowed.

"Book of Veles!" Reyna shouted.

In the distance, Officer Senko muttered the words into the phone.

Above her, the egg vibrated audibly. The wings tried to stretch further, but brushed up against a curved, invisible barrier. The moment contact was made, her nullygons on the ground sang frantically, working overtime to nullify the growing power. Drops of white light fell upwards into the sky.

She took out the container with the Mexican jumping bean, opened the lid, and watched it spin. Then she picked it up between her fingers, smelled it, and took the tiniest lick.

"Clockwise, almonds, spicy," she said.

The wings pushed harder against the invisible barrier, and Reyna saw the way they pressed, curved and flattened against it. The musculature flexed, and a burst of light came from the ground, from her nullygons. They were about to outlive their usefulness.

She debated picking them up to try and salvage some of her expenses, but it was too late. One of them burst into pink flame, and suddenly that was a four-thousand dollar claim she'd have to write up. With the circuit broken, the rest would no longer function, but at least they were physically intact. Their lights faded, they reverted to their inert, inactive shapes. She grabbed a few within reach and pocketed them.

She pulled the string with the crystal from her pocket, watched the stone surge upwards like a piece of metal attracted to the giant magnet that was the egg. She rotated the stone in her hands, waiting for details she needed to penetrate her thoughts.

"One thousand one hundred and twelve," she shouted, putting the stone back in the bag. "Is that enough? What do I get?"

"It's processing!" Senko said.

And then the thing with four wings flexed, uttering a deep, mournful cry. Its wings folded in, then unfurled.

Reyna took the hit and flew.

She had the good sense to tuck her bag against her like a baby and endured the constant litany of "OWOWOWOW" as she hit the top of a tree. It was enough to kill her speed.

She fell hard in an arc of descent, felt the breath knocked out of her, and rolled to a halt on the ground.

Gasping, she winced at the pain, something in the ribs. Well, that wasn't good. Her eyes were shut, but she rolled over as she heard the footsteps of Senko and a harried, "Oh *fuck,* are you okay?"

She was not, but it was one of those things people had to ask.

"Say..." she managed to gasp out.

"What?"

"Phone..."

Senko consulted the phone which should have spit out some kind of search result with all the input she'd inadvertently been giving it. "I don't even know how to pronounce this. Sim... argh... ill?"

"Simargl..." Reyna forced her eyes open and turned back towards the egg.

A back rose up, showing the wings firmly attached, then a head, a vast, dog-shaped head, followed by paws that stepped down onto the ground.

Reyna gestured towards the phone, and Officer Senko nearly dropped it into her hand like it was contagious. She read the details from her app.

Simargl. Celestial hound, prisoner of Polaris, mate of Kupalnitsa and held in check by the Daughters of the Dawn, the Zoryas.

Only the dog that was stepping down now, looking from one wing to the other, scratching at the ground experimentally, could not be a war dog of the apocalypse. Too small.

And despite what Reyna had said earlier, Senko—though she

couldn't really blame her—had gone back to readying her firearm. She wasn't aiming it, though, which probably meant she was still keeping a cool head about this.

At least, Reyna had a much better idea of what she was dealing with. But that didn't help her now as the giant, four-winged celestial dog tilted its head in that universal way that indicated it was trying to decide whether Reyna was a friend or a treat.

Reyna tried getting back on her feet, felt the wave of dizziness and the pain in her chest, and settled for getting to all fours. Senko helped her as she reached towards her bag. She heard the low pitched whine, turned her eyes towards the is-it-or-isn't-it-Simargl, and watched it take cautious, but not fearful steps, towards her.

"Seashells," Reyna said, holding up two fingers. "In the bag. *Go.*" She gestured towards both her bag and some general, vaguely safe distance away from her, and Senko, God bless her, got it immediately, picked up the bag, and ran off.

She wondered whether she should be touched that Senko trusted her enough to be okay that she ran without hesitation, or annoyed that this meant Senko had already written her off as a goner.

It all became sort of parenthetical to the fact that a giant spectral, celestial dog had lowered its giant nose and was sniffing and pushing against her like she was a chew toy someone had just dropped in the yard.

Realm 1112 put the Big Dog God Thing within the general Realm 1100 area code, not quite Earth, but at least Earth adjacent. She reached into her pocket and felt the smooth, still-warm metal of one of her nullygons and swiped a search pattern on it, homing in on the appropriate frequency. It was better than nothing.

It also saved her life as the nullygon chimed in her pocket, acknowledging her adjustment, and Simargl Jr. bit down. It lifted her into the air, held between its teeth like a book, rather than masticating her spleen in the opening, experimental bites of a new chew toy.

"I found them," she heard from what she could tell was a safe, respectful distance away. That was the sensible thing, but it created a problem with safely getting the shells into her hand.

"Throw the gun away," Reyna shouted back. At least it would be good for something that way.

"Do… do you mean fetch?"

"Yes!"

Reyna hoped Officer Senko had a competitive streak. If the woman without training was okay with being snapped up in the jaws of an ethereal beast, then the cop should be able to handle throwing a shiny object to distract it.

Her question was answered when even she winced at a high pitched whistle. She didn't even need to crane to look in the direction, her entire body moved towards the source as the dog turned its head.

Senko was waving the shiny, metallic pistol.

Reyna's stomach went queasy as her body moved up and down with the loping motion as captor headed towards the new toy.

"*Shit!*" Senko hissed as she threw the gun. She'd clearly hit the limit of her nerve with a massive, spectral demon dog thing bearing down on her.

Still, it had the intended effect. The dog jigged hard to follow the direction of the gun and dropped Reyna. She moaned as she hit the ground from a great height. Again. A sensation she was entirely too familiar with. God bless Canadian healthcare.

She was already holding her hand out when Senko placed the seashells there. Small things. Absolutely ordinary in appearance. She placed them against the nullygon that had saved her life, listened for the confirmation chime, and then put one in her mouth, keeping it in her cheek, like a hamster, while she kept the other near her ear.

"Help me up," she said around the shell in her mouth.

Senko offered her hand, and Reyna had no shame or hesitation about leaning hard into it. Even by her standards, she'd gotten kicked around a lot for this early in the morning. She ran her fingers up and down her right side and felt the soreness there.

Simargl Jr. came loping back, a contradiction of physics as the beast was absolutely huge but created no tremors as it returned.

Beside her, Senko swallowed hard.

Reyna held her hand up. *Do you understand me now?*

The dog skidded to a halt, its eyes wide.

YES.

You aren't Simargl.

I AM HIS SON.

And he sat down, tilting his head as he looked down at Reyna.

YOUR WORDS MAKE SENSE NOW.

I had to find the right channel. You understand you aren't meant to be here? You gestated in that egg. For decades. Feeding on the light of the dawn. I think someone wanted to take you away and unleash you since your father is imprisoned.

ARE THEY COMING FOR ME?

They've been… delayed. And I came for you instead.

WHY?

To find out what should be done next.

AND WHAT SHOULD BE DONE NEXT?

You can't stay here. But you haven't done anything wrong either.

"You know everything you say right now sounds like that Guild Navigator from Lynch's *Dune* movie, right?" Senko interrupted.

"Oh, is *that* what it sounds like without the shells? Huh. What does the dog sound like?"

"A Swedish subwoofer."

She turned back to the dog.

I have a temporary solution if you're agreeable. You need sanctuary.

She went back for her bag and pulled out more of the nullygons, then her most prized possession. She held it up in front of Senko. "Thank God for duct tape, huh?"

I need you to keep your head down and close, please.

He did it.

Good boy!

His tail thumped behind him, and his wings shivered. Reyna went up to his neck and held up a nullygon.

"Help me with this."

"What are you…"

She took the duct tape and laid it on, then put another nullygon on that. She hoped it would at least last long enough to prevent Simargl Jr. from laying waste to this corner of the dimension.

"No way. Really?"

"Every dog needs a collar."

Between the two of them, and with the beast's cooperation, they managed to space out the remaining nullygons around its neck at roughly even intervals.

This is going to feel a little weird.

She got a single nod in response, and she went ahead, configuring the nullygons. As she keyed each one in, Simargl Jr. shrank, losing his wings, becoming solid, becoming fluffy, and shedding his size and mass until he looked like a very healthy, but not necessarily show-dog quality purebred keeshond.

Reyna got on her knees, surveyed her handiwork, and then, just to be on the safe side, wrapped up the now shrunken nullygon collar in a few more layers of duct tape.

"Who's a good boy?" she asked.

The keeshond thunked his tail up and down rapidly, and Reyna stuck her hand out. It was immediately licked.

Officer Senko looked like someone had hit her on the back of the head with a pie. "What the hell did I just see?"

"I'm hungry. Are you hungry? I'm totally hungry. Where can I get coffee and breakfast? Nothing fancy, my treat."

"Why did I even come down here?"

"I told you I needed help." She reached into one of her pockets and pulled out a piece of paper. "Also, I need you to sign this."

"What is this?"

"A witness statement. You can hold onto it if you want before signing, but essentially it says you confirm you saw weird shit go down, and you weren't drunk when it happened."

"Who the hell are you with? CSIS?"

"No."

"CIA? Interpol?"

"Nothing that exotic, but I am an investigator."

"Okay, some crazy *X-Files* agency the world doesn't know about."

"Nah. Insurance."

Senko blinked. Simargl Jr. licked her hand, but she didn't appear to notice.

"What?"

Reyna pulled out her card and handed it over. It had her name and contact details under the company name Anomalous Adjustments.

"I'm an independent insurance adjuster. A client wanted to make sure they weren't getting faked out on a policy, and that they were entitled to coverage." She looked down at Simargl Jr. and patted his head. "I would say a big demon dog falls under the policy."

"For what kind of insurance?"

"The kind only the very rich and powerful can afford. Especially when they mess with forces they shouldn't, but still don't want to pay for it when a building comes down," she said. "The list is bigger than you'd think."

"And shrinking the demon dog down?"

"That's pro bono."

Senko shook her head. "Did you still want a cigarette?"

Reyna's head nodded hard enough to bounce her hair.

Senko obliged and offered her one.

She took it and placed it in her mouth. "Thanks."

Senko held out a lighter and Renya leaned in and accepted the flame. The first inhalation of the cigarette seared her throat in a comforting, familiar way.

"I should probably not be driving." Reyna turned and walked back to the police car. "Come on," she said to Simargl Jr.

He barked once and trotted beside her.

"You too," she said, over her shoulder to Senko.

She didn't wait to see if Senko would follow.

She leaned against the trunk. The dog sat beside her, panting. The cigarette smoke warmed and wafted in her throat. The reds, oranges, and yellows of the sun bled bright and warm in the morning sky. She keyed Jeff Beck's "Where Were You" from her phone's playlist and watched the sky lighten for a while.

The car beeped as Senko returned, unlocking the doors with the fob in her hand. "Had to get my gun."

Reyna opened the rear door and Simargl Jr. hopped in, happy to be there, tail thumping against the seat. Reyna took the passenger seat.

"Do you like pancakes?" Senko asked, getting into the driver's seat.

"You will arrest me in about ten minutes for murdering them," she said.

And they drove on.

BAUER SELECTS

Sheldon Birnie

There are only a few of us left hanging around when the rink rat who cleans the dressing rooms pokes his bald head in and gives us the ten-minute warning. A lull falls over the damp, sweaty room as a final round of cold ones are cracked.

"Hey Del," Barry belches, breaking the silence. "You ever tell the boys here about ol' Eddie?"

"Nah," I grumble, waving his suggestion away half-heartedly. "These guys don't wanna hear nothing like that."

"What's this?" Johnsy asks as he pulls on his drawers and plops back down onto the bench to sip his fresh brew. "You holdin' out on us Del?"

"Come on," Barry needles with a wink and a grin. "Let's hear it. Gotta finish up these pops, anyhow."

Now, I've told the story plenty over the years, late nights in the dressing room or early mornings sitting in a boat waiting on the fish to bite. It ain't a happy story, though.

"You boys sure? This ain't no heartwarmer, let me warn ya."

The boys all egg me on.

I steal a glance into the case of Busch Lights left standing by the garbage can in the middle of the room. There are a couple more holding it down. If we run late, we can always leave the rink rat a pop or two for keeping him there so late on a weeknight. He might cuss us out, but he'd forgive us. I take a long sip off my beer and sit back.

"Alrighty then."

○

I used to skate with a group of guys out of the old Manawaka Memorial Arena, a few years before the roof caved in on her back in '97. Good group of guys, lots of laughs, and even a couple decent hockey players in the mix, too. Not unlike you lot, only with better legs and full heads of hair.

Back then, there was a guy by the name of Eddie Franklin who'd lace up with us every Thursday night. Eddie was a nice enough guy, sure. He wasn't great shakes or nothing, but he was another body you could depend on, and he almost always brought beer. He was built like a brick shit house, too; you couldn't get him off the puck without a bit of muscle. But he didn't move too fast out there on his feet. Not until that final season he played with us, when he got them new-to-him skates, that is.

They were pretty banged up, heavier by far than anything you'd find new on the market these days, and they was held together by mismatched rivets, shoe goo, and a pair of frayed red and black laces that he never did get around to swapping out. Sure, they didn't smell so great, but them Bauer Selects fit Eddie just right and his old pair of CCMs were in even worse condition. So Eddie figures, what the hell.

"Blades were rusted something fierce," I recalled him saying, as he showed them off for the first time. "Nothing a good sharpen couldn't cure, though."

Course, Eddie never knew them skates was haunted, cursed or worse when he bought 'em, else he probably never would've paid the forty bucks for 'em in the first place.

First skate of the year, you could tell something was different with Eddie. He was just zipping around out there like a bat outta hell, even in warm-up. Come game time, Eddie's hungry for that puck. Starving, even. Usually, he'd follow the play—try to make the safe move. But now, boy, he's after that puck like it owes him money. A nice change, sure, if somewhat outta character. Little urgency ain't a bad thing, right?

But then, all of a sudden you can't get Ed off the ice, neither. And that wasn't never the case before. Sure, he'd get caught out on a bad change now and then. We all do. Some—lookin' at you Barry—more than others eh? But it wasn't never a problem before, neither. Now, though, Eddie don't never want to get off the ice. We'd have to holler at him and rattle that gate like hell each time he come zipping by and hope to Christ his ears was open.

"Sorry boys," Eddie'd say, dropping to the bench all red faced and outta breath, panting like a lumber cat in heat. "Feet've got a dang mind of their own over here."

Eddie kept up that way, too, as the season went on. We'd rib him hard, and he'd apologize up and down, but nothing'd change. He was even playing different out there. Eddie'd always been active on the rush and quick to back check, but like most of us, it wouldn't be wrong to say he could lack any real sense of urgency before then, particularly during those late-night ice times.

But now Eddie's charging after the puck, flying into the corners, Lord help anyone in his way. It was like something had got into him. The refs took notice, too. Big time. There's Eddie, who'd never logged more than the odd accidental tripping minor, sitting in the sin bin every game, knees bouncing in the box the whole while, anxious to get out and get moving again.

"Here he is," the boys'd chide when he set himself down in the dressing room after each game. "Lookin' a lot like Tiger Williams out there, Eddie!"

"Sorry boys," he'd say with a shake of his head. "Can't seem to catch a break with the stripes these days."

Then he'd pull his jersey over his head, crack a beer, and sit there, belly hanging out with his skates laced up. Matter of fact, Eddie'd gone from being one of the first guys up and outta the room to dang near the last each night. And it wasn't like he was showering up and lingering till the beer ran out. No, he'd just sit there, skates on, just kicking it till the next team came by to use the room or the rink rat gave us the boot, then pull his gear off lickety-split and head home, sweaty as could be. He'd leave them Selects on long as he could, too.

It was around that time, must have been early October, before the weather really turned cold, that I got my first indication that something was up with Ed. I'd got out of the shower, was lounging in my towel while he was still fully dressed. He said he'd got himself into a regular Wednesday evening pickup game over Minnedosa way.

"Right on," I tells him. "Really getting your money's worth for them new skates, eh?"

"Sure, sure," was all he says. "Can't get enough, these days."

I didn't think much of it, until I was chatting with him a few weeks later—coulda been a month maybe, I don't recall, exactly. When I asked him how it was going with them pickup games, his eyes bugged out again.

"Good," he says. "Found myself a regular Monday evening game up in Dauphin, too."

"Christ," I says, figuring between the 'Dosa and Dauphin games, old Eddie's really putting the miles on his old F-150. I says as much to him, but he just shrugged.

"Yeah," Eddie says. "But what the hell. Gotta scratch the itch, right?"

Heck, there's nothing wrong with driving all over the Parkland to play pickup hockey. But the look in Eddie's eyes and the way he'd been acting on the ice made me feel like something was going on with ol' Ed. Something strange.

See, Eddie's antics on the ice had only increased, too. He wasn't just running after the puck, but running guys into the boards and generally making a menace of himself. One night, right around that time, he even got himself thrown out of a game. He'd never done nothing like that before. No way, no how.

"Jeez, Ed," I says after we all get off the ice twenty minutes later. "What the hell's gotten into ya?"

Eddie, he's sitting there with his sweater and shoulder pads off, but he hasn't touched his skates.

"Sorry, boys," he says, sounding like a broken record. "I dunno what happened. Kinda lost it out there, I guess."

"No shit, Sherlock," some joker says. "Tell us somethin' we don't fuckin' know."

But Eddie just shakes his head. I noticed then that he'd lost weight. Used to be Eddie's gut would hang out over his Coopers, but no more. Wasn't surprising, considering all the skating he was doing. But Eddie still had that crazy look in his eye, too. Sunk back into his head as they was like he was some sorta Halloween goblin. When most of the guys had showered and headed home, Eddie was still sitting there, half-undressed and looking regretful. After I towelled off, I grabbed a couple cold ones from the open cases in the middle of the room and sat myself down next to Ed.

"You alright, bud?" I asks him. "Something eatin' ya?"

He took the Coors I handed him without a word and cracked it.

"Shit, buddy," Ed says after taking a long pull off his Colorado Kool-Aid. "Guess I ain't been sleeping much."

"Work?" I asks. "How's things at home?"

"Nah," he shrugs. "Work's work. Same shit as always. Home's the same. Only... It's like, when I try to sleep each night, it's like I can't stop thinking about the last game. Or the next one. And when I do sleep, I'm dreaming I'm chasing the goddamn puck down the ice and the rink is like a dark tunnel that goes on and on and on forever. It's fucked, I know, but..."

Eddie trailed off, then, and took a long pull off his pop. I did the same. What else could I do? I figured there must have been more going on with Eddie, behind the scenes, but I've never been one to pry. Especially not in the dressing room after a tough loss. So I let it slide.

I missed the next couple ice times—out of town for work for one, sick for the second—but when I returned to the rink in early December, Eddie looked even worse, run ragged and then some. He took a couple penalties that evening, but managed to keep his cool, more or less, if I recall correctly. When we got to talking, after the game, I asks him how things was going out in 'Dosa and up in Dauphin.

"Stopped going," he says, dropping his eyes. "Too much driving. Been hitting up the ODR two, three nights a week, though. Ain't the same, but she's worth it just to get out for a skate."

"Sure," I says, not thinking nothing of it.

Found out later that Eddie'd been asked not to come back out to either the 'Dosa or the Dauphin games. Seems his new-found attitude on the ice was rubbing the regulars the wrong way. Truth be told I wasn't terribly surprised. But never having known Eddie to lie, though, it seemed kinda weird that he didn't just tell me the truth. Guess he was embarrassed, and rightly so. Again, I never asked Eddie about it, though I've often wished I had.

Talk about missing one hundred percent of the shots you don't take, eh?

○

"Did Gretzky really say that?" Johnsy asks. "Or is that, like, an urban myth or whatever?"

The boys all groan. Barry tosses a tape ball across the room, which bounces off his shoulder. These young guys, sometimes they ain't so sharp upstairs.

"Jeez, just asking boys," Johnsy says. "Cool it, cool it. Sorry Del."

I wave off the boy's apology, take the opportunity to wet my whistle, gather my thoughts. It's been a while since I talked about ol' Ed, though I don't reckon there's an ice-time that goes by that I don't think of the poor guy.

"Now," I says, making a show of setting my beer down. "Where was I?"

○

Over the holidays, the lake froze over. Not that it didn't every winter, but this year, considering we didn't have much of nothing by way of snowfall, the entire lake froze clear and solid and smooth as a skating rink.

It was incredible, one of them once or twice in a lifetime sorta things. Games of shinny were going round the clock it seemed, down by the main beach, while people passed the puck and played games of keep-away that stretched out the length of football fields across that crisp, clear ice. You could skate from shore to shore, unfettered by boards or snowdrifts or anything but the odd crack to hop over here and there.

I was out there the afternoon of New Year's Eve with the wife and the kids all bundled up, just puttering about and having some fun. Christ, it was cold as cold could be, but there was dozens of folks out there, too, bundled up as we was and making the most out of it.

Eddie was one of them.

We was catching a quick breather, about a half a mile out from shore, about to make our way back in to call it a day and grab a hot chocolate, when he skated up out of the bright reflection of the low winter sun. I raised a gloved hand and hollered, "Hey Ed!"

"Del," Eddie wheezes, out of breath and then some as he hit the brakes, cutting a wide swoop in to stop up next to us. "Didn't see ya there in the glare!"

I got a good look at him then, as he stood there sucking wind. He was sweating, despite the cold. And while his face was red raw from the wind and the exertion, the tips of his ears and the bridge of his nose was frozen white.

"Ya got yourself a touch a frostbite there, Ed," I says.

"Really?" Eddie says, wiping his forehead. "Jeez, I'm just sweating buckets. You can really pick up some steam out there in the open."

"No kidding," I says. "But you're gonna lose an inch of ear if you keep it up, bud."

Eddie shook his head, blinked a few times, as though in a daze. Then his eyes seemed to focus on something off in the distance, out in the middle of the frozen lake.

"Sure, Del," he says, before taking a couple strides towards shore. "Nice running into ya."

We headed on in ourselves after that. I didn't think of Eddie again until I seen him at the rink a few days later. By then, he's got the look of a red raccoon, face wind-burned and frostbit around the eyes, and his ears was bright as Christmas ornaments.

"Cripes, Ed," I says with a whistle. "Wind done bitya something fierce, eh?"

"Yeah," Ed says, all sheepish, sitting there in his skates a half hour before icetime. "Didn't feel like nothing when I was out there. But I guess I got 'er pretty good…"

"Darn tootin' ya did, dummy," some joker chimed in. The boys all laughed, of course. Looking back now, though, I can tell ya that shoulda been a big red goal buzzer flashing to let us know that things wasn't right with ol' Eddie, not one bit. Instead, we just got dressed and hit the ice like every other night.

It wasn't long after that we all learned that Eddie and his gal, Laurenna, had split. Word on the street was that things hadn't been going well for a while, and it all kind of fell apart over the holidays. I never got a chance to ask her about it, so I can't rightly say what happened between them. All's I know is it was a sad mess, the whole damn thing.

Course, that is neither here nor there. Fact remains that by the time February rolled around, Laurenna had her own place across town, while Eddie kept living in the house they'd once shared. He kept looking worse, too—thinner—his beer belly shrinking until it didn't even hang over his pants anymore. At the time we put it all down to a case of the blues. A few of the boys had been in similar situations, so they took to him in the dressing room, going out for beers after the game or tagging along with him for a little skate or shinny session.

Eddie took to spending more and more time out on the ice, and not just down at the community centre ODR, but hitting up the big lake on the daily, too. The municipality'd clear off a big old patch along the lakefront for folks to keep skating on. Others, and I reckon Eddie was one of them, even cleared paths and little shinny sheets further out onto the lake.

Who could blame the guy?

Problem was Ed had developed a tendency to get out on the ice when he had no business being there. One night, during a bitter cold front at the end of February, the kind of cold where trees pop and the ice screeches beneath your blades, Eddie went out and done frost bit his ears so bad he lost parts of both of 'em.

Now, I only seen Eddie alive again one more time after that, and he wasn't looking too good, let me tell ya. Fact, he looked downright haggard. Both ears—what was left of 'em, anyways—was all swole up something fierce. His face was gaunt from the weight he'd lost, bags dark as pucks under his ghostly blue eyes.

"Tough luck, Ed," I tells him, when I stopped by his place to see him. "Doing okay?"

"Sure, sure," Ed says. "Tough luck for the boys last week, too, I heard."

Our season had just ended, with a loss in the first game of our winner-takes-all-playoff, while Ed had been shut up in hospital, and we wouldn't be back on the ice until late September.

"We'll get 'em next year," I says, before cutting to the quick of things. "What the heck were ya doing out there, bud?"

Ed shrugged and took a moment to answer, staring at the table while he put his thoughts together.

"It was like I was dreaming," he says finally, looking me in the eyes. "It felt good to skate. But it was also like I just… had to. Like I had no choice. The more I'd push, the harder I'd go. Harder I'd go, the lighter I felt. I'd be charging up the ice, just skating, not even chasing the puck or nothing, I just kept skating and skating and skating and that felt like it was enough."

I didn't say nothing. What was there to say?

"That might not make sense," Ed says with a sad, empty chuckle. "But that's how it is. Or was, I guess. You follow me, Del?"

"Sure, Ed," I says, and I thought I did, too. I put it down to the ordeal and the hard times the winter had brought his way, that skating was a way he could put all them troubles behind him and just be. But I reckon there was more to it than that, now. "I hear ya. Now you rest up and get better, eh? We need ya good and healthy next season."

"Sure thing, Del," Ed says, though he don't look at me when he says it. Instead, he's looking off over my shoulder, out the window into the dark night. Towards the lake. "I'll do that."

Of course, he didn't do no such thing. Two weeks later, Eddie was dead.

○

"Jesus Christ," Johnsy curses softly, leaning his head back against the damp cinderblock wall of the dressing room. "I heard about a guy who drowned skating on the lake back when I was in high school. Never knew you guys knew the guy."

"That we did," Barry confirms, taking a slow step up off the bench to grab a final cold one from the case. He tosses one across to Johnsy before sitting himself back down. "Hell of a guy, too."

"You ain't shitting, are ya, Del?" Johnsy asks, as though I'd string him along with as sad a story as this one.

"No sir," I tell him.

"Goddamn."

The rest of the boys all sit there, saying nothing. Either they heard this one before or they heard enough of it to know how she turns out. I just shake my head slow, take a long pull off my cold one before finishing up.

○

Considering the time of year, Eddie had no business going out on the lake again. Sure, it may have looked frozen solid, but any idiot knows that ain't the case once the snows start melting. Even though there weren't no open water, there's weak spots and thin spots, and Eddie done hit one of 'em but good.

Of course, everyone was just devastated. We'd all seen Eddie sliding downhill and it felt like we'd failed him. There was some folks who even talked like it was a suicide. Not that there was ever a note or nothin' found. Going out on the ice in the early spring, like he done, don't speak much to good sense, and it does lend itself to the idea that Eddie certainly wasn't in his right mind at the time, death wish or not.

No one knows how long Eddie was out there, striding and looping and gliding across the ice on Lake Manawaka that night, but I like to imagine he was out there as long as he needed to be, taking in the majesty of the cosmos above, at peace with himself and whatever it was that was haunting him right before the crack and splash and the thrashing terror that must have followed. But I ain't so sure that's the case.

Over the years, on those nights when sleep just won't come, I've thought long and hard on Eddie's final season with us. Like how he wasn't himself on the ice, but that the ice was the one place he kept coming back to, hoping to find something. Like how he felt like he was dreaming out there, skating out in the cold. And how the harder he skated, the lighter he felt.

Again and again, I think of the haunted look in his eyes.

They held Eddie's funeral the Saturday after he drowned. All the boys went, of course. Afterwards, we took over the back room at the Legion and got right into it as *Hockey Night in Canada* wound through its double-header. At some point into the second game, after the pints had been swapped for tumblers full of rye whiskey and dark rum, a couple of the guys got talking in hushed tones about some of the grimmer details around Eddie's "death by misadventure," as the local coroner had dubbed it.

Someone driving down the lake road had seen Eddie out there on the ice. They'd hightailed it over to The Dock, where the lounge was still open, pulled in and got the bartender to call the fire department for him.

"Buddy's just hollerin', 'There's a maniac way out on the ice, skating,'" Hammy, a volunteer firefighter who used to skate with us now and then, was telling the boys. "So we load up and head out. No sign of him when we get down to the lake, but we get set up and soon enough we're out there, working our way further and further from the shore till we come up on it. The hole."

By then, the local Mounties were on the scene, too, cruisers lined up with the firetruck and an ambulance, lights flashing along the shoulder of the lake road. It didn't take them much fishing around before they landed on poor Eddie, hauling his lifeless body up out of those frigid depths.

"It was sad as hell," Hammy says, shaking his head before downing the rest of his rye. Then he sets the empty glass down on the bar and waves for another. "What gets me most, knowing him and all, is that he didn't have no skates on when we hauled him up. No socks neither. Poor bastard was barefoot as the day he was born."

The reason they give for the missing skates and socks? Eddie must have kicked 'em loose as he thrashed about, trapped under the ice and weighed down by his soaking wet winter clothes. Me, though? I don't buy it. No way, no how.

Anyone who ever sat next to Eddie in the dressing room knew the man tied his skates tight as he could stand 'em, pulling on them frayed old laces until he was red in the face. Unless he had the wherewithal to reach down through the deep, dark waters and unlace 'em as he sank, holding his breath all the while, there's just no way those skates shimmied themselves loose. I ain't disputing the fact that those skates were missing when they pulled him up onto the ice not a half hour after he fell through. I just don't know that there's a rational explanation for it.

What do I believe? Well, boys, I've said it before, and I'll say it again: those Bauer Selects Eddie had were haunted, cursed or worse. By whom or what, I can't rightly say. But I tell ya, they wasn't right.

Come the fall of that year, after the kids had gone back to school, but before the rink was up and running for the season, I found myself in the sporting goods shop down on Main Street, which at the time was the one place in town where you could find decent used gear. I was looking for some shoulder, shin and elbow pads for my son, who was just starting Atoms back at that time. As I was making my way to the back, where the kids' stuff was stored, glancing at the shelves of skates as I passed by, I caught sight of something that stopped me dead in my tracks. My mouth dropped open, slack, and I got a run of goosebumps from my heels up to the back of my head, which was pretty well bald even way back then.

Sitting there on the shelf were them Bauer Selects. They was just as banged up as the last time I seen Eddie lace 'em up, with the swear-to-Christ exact same pair of frayed, mismatched red and black laces that he never did get around to swapping out. The only difference was the blades, which were rusted all to hell. Not, I recalled with a chill despite the balmy weather and lack of air conditioning, unlike how Eddie'd described them when he first come across them Selects himself a year earlier.

"Where'd you get these skates?" I hollered at Jimbo, the shop owner. I couldn't bring myself to touch 'em, to pick 'em up and take 'em to the counter, so I waited, skin crawling, heart hammering in my chest like I'd just got off the ice after getting caught deep in our own end for a long shift, while Jim limped on back into the racks.

"Those rusty old things?" Jimbo says when he finally shuffled up next to me. He scratched at his chin, and his ample belly, mulling it over for a minute. "Couldn't rightly tell ya. Pretty sure they been sitting right there for years."

I opened my mouth to tell old Jimbo he was wrong, but what was I gonna say? That them skates shoulda been thirty feet underwater on the bottom of Lake Manawaka rather than on the shelf of his shop? That he should just up and burn 'em, haunted, cursed or worse as they was?

No. I didn't say nothing. I just clapped my mouth shut, paid for the gear I needed and got the hell outta there.

○

Right about then, the old rink rat sticks his head in the dressing room again.

"OK, boys," he says as he shuffles in and begins sweeping at the tape balls and empty cans that had missed the garbage can. "Wrap it up here, for cryin' out loud."

"Sure thing, pal," I say, draining the dregs of my beer and tossing the empty into the bin. It's past midnight and my 6:30 a.m. alarm isn't getting any farther away. I stand up and stretch, take my coat off the peg on the wall behind me and start pulling it on. I nod to the nearly empty case next to the trash. "Help yourself there, eh?"

The rink rat stops what he's doing and shuffles over to the case. After reaching in, popping the top, he stops to listen, sipping and waiting for the rest of the guys to get up, pull on their own coats and mitts and shoulder their bags.

"Now, I still don't have a hot clue as to how those skates got from the bottom of the lake to old Jimbo's shop there, but I'm sure they did just that," I continue, hoisting my own battered bag over my shoulder. "I seen 'em there with my own two eyes, and even though I'm pushing sixty, I still don't need glasses to read the sports pages. What's worse, I don't know where those skates was before Eddie found them in that exact same spot the year before. But I do know that when the lake's frozen solid, covered in snow as it most often is, and the wind takes to howling something fierce those nights in darkest February, I think of Eddie out there, just skating and skating and skating into the darkness. And then skating some more. And I wonder who or what it was that was pushing him on. I don't rightly reckon I'll ever know. What's worse, I'm not so sure I'd even want to, if I did."

"Man," mutters Johnsy, who's sitting there with his head in his hands. "That's fucked. I'm sorry, boys."

"Don't sweat it," Barry says, stretching before shouldering his own bag. "Let's hit the road here though, eh?"

We all decamp, shuffling through the dingy hall beneath the weight of our bags and sticks, the damp old smell of the rink trailing us out the doors like the ghosts of ten thousand forgotten games. Crossing the parking lot, I wave to the boys before looking up at the full moon shining through the clouds. I wonder, not for the first time and surely not the last, just where those Bauer Selects ended up in the end. I shiver just a little more than the crisp air would warrant, thinking of the cold waters of Lake Manawaka. I hope to Christ I never find out.

THOSE WHO FLOAT ON CURRENTS OF EARTH

Premee Mohamed

At midnight, the dry land broke like a bone.

Fielding, operating on muscle memory from school drills, dove from his bed, snatched his phone from its charger, and ran outside before he had fully woken. Warm darkness, extravagant stars. The low rumble of an engine somewhere abruptly cut off. The stones of their front lawn jealously guarded the day's heat and he skittered across them to the cool sidewalk, waiting for his parents to emerge. Under the swaying streetlight, the road shimmered with thousands of grasshoppers fleeing their burrows.

The neighbours sleepily came out one by one, clutching squirming cats or dozing toddlers, and waved to Fielding. He waved back.

It wasn't much of a quake. More of a *shake*, he thought. Where had he gotten the idea that something had broken, and badly? Dreamily he kept thinking of his leg two summers ago, that clean sharp wrongness on the X-ray.

Text messages began to pop up from his best friend: *MyFrac says 5.5*, followed by a dozen jiggling eyeballs, a nod to the Foolproof Earthquake Detection System they'd put up in their rooms: two plastic googly eyes glued to a piece of red construction paper.

He checked his and wrote back *5.4 here.*

Not so bad, she wrote. *LOL.*

Not so bad.

○

In the morning, they met at the edge of town in what Sparrow insisted on calling their secret fort—a metering shack for a long-defunct battery of oil wells, barely bigger than a backyard shed, the lightly corrugated walls rusted right through and admitting wet streaks of light below the diffuse glow of the small, smeared window.

Fielding rubbed his chest, frowning. Something still felt broken, though he hadn't been hurt in the quake. He could not place it within his body, nor outside, exactly. And Sparrow was agitated too, jiggling her foot and shaking her wrist as if she were charging her watch, whose green dot in the darkness told him it was already at a hundred percent. Today she was just like her name, the light fearless body seemingly hollow-boned under the drab plumage of her T-shirt and khakis, face feathered with freckles.

"I don't wanna stick around town today," she announced. "Do you? You don't really, do you? Let's go somewhere."

"Where?"

"I came up with the idea, now you have to come up with the place."

Something's wrong, he wanted to say. *Isn't it?* Around her he felt stodgy, slow, heavy. The hulk of a rusting tractor around which livelier creatures hopped and fought. She feared nothing but boredom, he thought. But she must feel *something* this morning.

"Okay," he said after a minute. They had the rest of the summer to find strange places; today they could start somewhere familiar. Maybe that would be best after last night's shock. "The old plant?"

"Yes!"

Fielding put his bike on manual to refill the battery, and Sparrow grumblingly reset hers ("Why didn't you plug it in last night?") to keep pace; at a leisurely pedal they set off towards the long-defunct Genesee power station, a favourite though distant haunt.

Starved of coal, the mines around it no longer profitable, it had been mothballed for a decade but not shut down till at last the myriad lawsuits had tangled into a spiderweb and yanked out the remaining plugs. Barriers, bollards, spikes, and fences had been erected, clearly meant to keep out vehicles; it was a joy to sneak in with bikes.

And once inside, the secretive wonders of the dusty machinery, the dead screens, the satisfying clack of buttons and dials, whispering the names of equipment like a prayer, swinging from the hanging chains.

They pulled in at the side of the highway after half an hour to drink snack-sized bottles of warm kefir from their backpacks, over Fielding's protestations.

"What's it going to do?" said Sparrow, grimacing as she swallowed hers. "I mean, it's just bacteria, right. It'll just get more bacteria-y."

"Yeah, till it turns into cheese."

"No it *won't.* It'll just turn into yogurt."

Fielding's bottle (raspberry-blueberry) fizzed like a stolen mouthful of beer. *That* wasn't good, he was sure. He replaced his gogglemask and looked around, ignoring Sparrow's gagging and slurping.

June, hot, and everything with that hard golden light you had to filter out of your photos. Invisible dust hung high in the atmosphere, mixed with the ubiquitous wildfire smoke. Where was it blowing from now? He hadn't looked at the map on the way out. Shimmering in the far haze, the pale blades of wind turbines turned sluggishly, as if sick. Beautiful though, he thought, like upraised swords.

"Are you guys going to Ponoka this year?"

Sparrow wiped her mouth, leaving a muddy smear. "I don't think so. But I wanted to, because Ashlynn is riding, and..."

"Oh, that's cool," he said, as she trailed off; Sparrow was blushing hotly under her tan. You didn't talk about crushes, that was the rule. Some animal instinct of terror between them had prevented it all their lives, and now, at eleven, it was both on its way out and stronger than ever. "Baseball got cancelled, didn't it?"

"Yeah. I asked Mom to talk to the county, but..." She kicked at the gravel road, frustrated. "It's so *stupid*. Because of the Bracket or whatever."

Fielding nodded. Among the dozens of interesting fungal diseases that had arisen in the past twenty years, BRK-142 had become the most locally worrisome; it infected trees and shrubs, cereal and legume crops, but when the wind and the humidity and the heat were just right (or wrong, he supposed) the inhaled spores could kill people, too. And with the annual floods and fires, it roamed the place as excitedly as a lost dog, wild with freedom. Most outdoor sports had been moved inside, but not baseball, and Sparrow was the best junior pitcher for counties around. They'd done a news article about her in Edmonton, even.

"It's good anyway," she said abruptly, not looking at him. "Dad got fired last week."

"What?"

"Well not *fired*. Laid off."

"Shit. You never said."

The town was dying, jobs were hard to come by; they both knew that. It was in their bones, like the other countdown they could not help but think about. Once there had been coal and oil, and then just oil, and now it was mostly fracking and farming (barley, oats, the special drought-proof canola-mustard), in good summers. But both their dads worked in what remained of oil. That was supposed to be secure. They had already gotten rid of (in his dad's words) all the dead weight. Companies were light, mostly robots and computers, and the handful of supersmart staff that ran them.

"What are you guys gonna do?" Fielding said, pulling his gogglemask down again so she could see his face.

"I don't know. Mom says..." She stared across the dull olive of the fields around them, the humped shoulders of the river valley lined with dead trees turned the peculiar violet of infection. Then she shook her head sharply. "Mom says a lot of stuff. But look!"

She pointed, and he followed the line of her arm down to the valley, in which, like a glitched image, glassily bisected, a slump was clearly visible, all the layers of stone and soil as crisp as anything in a textbook.

"I wonder what else the quake did," Fielding said. The zoom on his phone wasn't very good, though the air was clearer near the river; the striations were running together. That would look crappy on Instagram. "I mean, what else we might see."

"Cool shit," Sparrow said. "I bet. The epicentre was right near the plant."

"Was it? Did you know that this morning?"

"Yeah. I wanted to see what you'd say though." She beamed at him. "Come on."

○

They paused twice more on the trip, once to let a small creek of ants rush across in front of them, perhaps escaping something, and once because Fielding's bike radar picked up a cloud that turned out to be American bees headed their way.

"They're swarming," Sparrow whispered as they huddled in a field of stunted and curled barley, a hundred yards from their bikes. "They won't sting."

"Okay, *you* go tell them that." The swarm roared, wailed, vortexed upwards in a long slender string, like a waterspout, then descended on their bikes; a moment later they were gone, a long cloud moving against the wind. "They never swarm in June."

"Weird. Maybe the earthquake screwed up their hive."

So much was unknown now, so much went unstudied; he knew that. Their textbooks, old even when his parents had studied in their small town, still showed blue sky, green stands of trees. It had snowed every winter, but didn't flood every spring. No mention of induced seismicity. Nothing about climate. Not even weather.

"What are you doing?"

Fielding dragged his hand from his chest and stuffed it into his pocket. "I don't know."

"Are you okay? Maybe we shouldn't have drunk that kefir," Sparrow said worriedly. "Wanna go back?"

"No, let's go. We're this far."

As they pulled up and lifted their bikes over the shin-high ring of concrete barriers, speech failed them for the first time that day.

For the entire plant was broken, clumsily, into a dozen huge shards, dust still rising from unseen places where a vent or pipe must have been fluting air into the wreckage. It resembled nothing so much as a great fallen corpse, like the photos you kept seeing of 'the last elephant' on TV, even though it never turned out to be the last.

"Wowwwwwww," Sparrow whispered, her face alight.

We shouldn't go in, Fielding almost said, but realized at once what he meant to say was that they must, because they were the first, and they were never the first at anything, or the first to *see* anything, and who else could have known the plant was like this today? The surveillance cams had been shut down long ago, and drones never came here, preferring to fly over the cities. He found he was shaking, his hands trembling as he raised his phone.

"We could, like," Sparrow began, then paused. "Sell pictures of this. Footage or whatever. Like, record it and…"

"What? Who'd buy that? They could just fly a camera out here."

"Yes, but ours would be first," she said, ignoring his flinch. "And *we* would have pics from inside. They'd never risk something in there. They're too expensive, the good ones. I mean the news ones."

"Oh, so we're gonna risk *ourselves* inside. After they told us a million times not to be under a roof during a quake."

"Sure," she said. "Kids are a dime a dozen."

"We are not a dime a dozen," he said indignantly. They had this fight about once a week. "We're like. *Precious* or whatever. *Valuable.*"

"Oh, screw what Mrs. Pedersen said. You don't even like her."

"Yeah, but..." *But what happens if we get killed?* he wanted to say.

Mrs. Pedersen said children were precious, the future. Mrs. Pedersen said a lot of things. But everybody else said, right around the time they were born: *The world has twelve years.* They didn't say what any of that meant. Not 'the world,' which would go on without Fielding or Sparrow; or 'has,' what it meant to 'have' a world. *But we've got less than a year left if they were right. What are we going to do after this? We can't just keep... goofing off forever. Biking out here and jumping around on the generators. Looking for old pumpjacks to see if there's any spilled manometer mercury to play with. And we're not even* supposed *to! We'll have to grow up, and you think you won't, and you don't even* care *if we die here, and...*

She was moving though, and he couldn't let her go in alone; he trotted after her, ready to interpose his slightly bigger body between her and anything that might be inside.

And here, the wrongness overcame him, washed over him like a wave; it was nearly a relief to have it pinpointed so precisely.

At his side, he became dimly aware that Sparrow had wrenched away her mask to gasp, hand over her mouth. For the floor was not merely cracked like the building's exterior, but right through and down, as neatly as a broken brick, exposing the strata of the thick stained cement above long ridges of soil and stone.

"It's... glowing."

"No it isn't," Sparrow said, and peered down into the closest corner of the gape. "Oh, wait. Um. Maybe we should..."

"It *is*, though."

"Um." She stuffed her phone into her pants pocket and zipped it up, then began to edge towards the centre of the hole, where the glow was strongest.

"Don't!" Fielding couldn't help shouting this time, and his chest hurt as if the bone there (*sternum, that's what they said*, he thought a little hysterically) were broken instead of the ground.

The noise of his shout echoed terrifyingly around the shell of the place, startling a couple of birds off the roof. Had he imagined the glow brightening? No, it couldn't be.

"I'm not going all the way down! Jeez." But she was, he could see that, the *liar*, and his fear froze him in place, clutching his phone to his aching chest. She added, "You're the one who always says to look before whatever."

"Before you *leap*."

"Well, I'm not leaping, so it doesn't even apply, technically. Crunch my balls." Her voice was fading and this frightened him even more than losing sight of her head, the curls disappearing below the edge of the broken cement.

He lunged for the opening, and slid down a short incline before bumping into her, so that they both wobbled and snatched at the walls, hitting their hands on bits of broken rebar.

"We're gonna get in so much trouble," he said.

"For what?"

"For, um." He paused, clinging to a broken copper pipe as she inched ahead of him. Trespassing, probably, but they'd been here dozens of times. Not theft. What else was there? "Well, remember last year when Brayden got stuck in that auger bin…"

"Oh, whatever. This is like a ramp. We can climb back up."

"What if we can't?"

"Well, I mean." She glanced back at him, a gleam of something catching her eye as if a coin had flipped. "I mean look at what's out there."

"Yeah. But what if we, like. What if it's radon or something?"

"You can't see radon. Anyway, what if we get superpowers?"

"You," he said patiently, "would use yours for *evil*."

"No I wouldn't. I'd be a hero. I'd fight…"

The future, he thought. *Our enemy*.

Sadly he inhaled, exhaled. Aside from Sparrow's usual odour of sunscreen and sweat, the air smelled strange: *clean*, he realized. No spores, no dust, no smoke. And the glow, so far from the red or orange he realized he had been expecting, was neither, but a soft, silvery blue.

He looked down at his feet: dusty faux-Nikes, with the swoosh squashed flat and going the wrong way. Steady on the sloped dirt. Below: darkness, and that silvery thread. *We can climb back up, can't we? But if we can't. Listen. If we can't. Then. Maybe it won't be so bad for… for the left-behind. For us, too. For the world. Maybe. And I can't leave her alone.*

He descended and breathed the clean air.

The disaster came in silence. Sparrow fell first, without a noise; Fielding tried to scream and produced only a faint whistling noise.

One moment she had been ahead of him, crisply silhouetted in the glow, talking about balrogs; the next, gone. And then the solid stone beneath his front foot had turned into air. The single image of her tensed back rushed through his head in the ten or fifteen seconds it took him to fetch up on solid ground again.

Are we dead? Did we die? We are *going to be in trouble.*

Slowly he raised himself and stared. If this was heaven, it was not as advertised: a flat plain, a slaty sky over lush bizarre grass, greener than the plastic stuff in the soccer arena. It felt soft nearly to the point of slimy under his hands, and he lifted them to stare at the twin bright smears on his palms.

Sparrow groaned and stood to frisk herself. "Oh my God," she said, staring up at the ominous sky. "We're dead. Right?"

"Maybe. I thought there'd be angels."

"I thought there'd be fire," she said, and laughed uncertainly, because it *was* sort of funny, but they *had* fallen: they both remembered falling. And if you fell more than a few seconds, you were dead, weren't you? And anyway, *if* they had survived such a long fall, even then you would not see this below the busted power plant, only darkness, and (Fielding thought, perhaps based on a video they had watched in science class) a red, molten-nickel glow, like the core of the earth. Or was it iron? He could not remember.

You were supposed to tell a teacher if you had thoughts like this, he did remember that. Like, *I dreamed I was dead.* Or, *I don't want to die. I just don't want to be alive any more.*

Or, *I just want to know what else there is than this.*

Absently, he groped for Sparrow's hand; she held it for a moment, and then dropped it, as if they had shaken on a deal, and they set off across the thick strange grass towards the only thing in the landscape.

This was a house, unfamiliar from TV or movies, and certainly unlike anything in their town, which tended toward squat, practical bungalows roofed with solar tiles in about five variations of brown and grey. This was a mansion, like from a book—white and high, a wedding cake with a high uneven roof and nothing around it: no driveway, no road, no fence.

The air smelled of grass and recent rain. The rough white exterior of the house seemed correspondingly dirty and wet, as if the rain had washed something dark from the shingles. A single window was lit with a rosy golden glow, like a miniature sunset.

"Maybe it's not Hell," Sparrow whispered. "Maybe it's like. Narnia."

"Maybe we're chosen ones."

"I don't *want* to be a chosen one."

"But we could save the kingdom," he pointed out, and paused on the doorstep, hand raised to knock. "If there's a kingdom."

"But I don't want to get bossed around. We could at *least* get some Turkish Delight," Sparrow said.

"Yeah. Unfermented or whatever."

"I bet you could make kefir out of Turkish..." she began, and trailed off as the door—black, deeply-panelled, and so glossy they could see their faces in it—swung open ahead of them.

Fielding glanced at her, trying to communicate without having to say it, *We could still go back. See where we fell. Retrace our steps... there wasn't a door, but there was a gate, I felt us pass through it...*

She shook her head as if he had spoken and followed him into the darkened interior, lit by distant reflections. Behind them the door clicked as it settled back into the jamb, clunked (unmistakably) as a lock shot home.

It's a trap, because of course it's a trap; but it's all a trap, isn't it? Fielding thought as they began to move down a slick, tile-floored hallway, the only path open to them. *Life, school, all of that. And outside this trap? If the world only has a year left? A year left of what? More traps? Different ones? Not freedom.*

May as well be trapped here. I hope we get less annoying though.

"There's supposed to be a witch," Fielding whispered. "In Narnia."

"I hope so," Sparrow said. "Then I could be a witch apprentice."

"Sparrow."

"A witch... what do you call it? Prestige?"

"Protégé."

"Yeah."

They moved softly through the house, glancing up at the dark wooden walls at dozens of paintings whose subjects seemed to be nothingness, only gilt frames surrounding clouds of grey and sepia, brush marks visible beneath the yellowing varnish. Doors closed behind them, sending them inexorably up (Fielding knew) towards the room in which someone, or something, had a light that was more like fire than electrons.

It was not a witch. Something told him: something that had told him just where and how the place he loved had broken.

And why do you love it anyway, he seemed to hear the closing doors hiss. *Why not love what is here instead: what is whole, what is wet, what is clean. Not that ugly place.*

I don't know. I don't know.

At last a final door closed, and Fielding shook his head, as if dashing water from his dry, fair hair. The trap sprung, jaws closed.

A low room, plaster ceiling, black beams of wood; a fireplace, from which the light they had seen emanated through a strange stained-glass window of rose and amber. But nothing burned inside: no logs, no tubes carrying captive gas. Just a flame trapped in a box; obedient, perhaps to the thing that sat next to it at a tall desk, in a swiveling wooden chair.

Welcome to this place. You are greatly welcome. For you two are my new apprentices. And it has been long ere I had even one.

"No, we're not," Sparrow whispered.

Fielding wondered how she could speak—what she was seeing. All he could see clearly was a squirming mass of something, which when he looked straight at it became a void that hurt his eyes, and when he looked away became a whitish light, pulsing like a heart. A witch? A wizard? Something else?

If they were dead, then it was a demon, or an angel, but he could not believe he was dead—not with his knees bruised from a fall of uncertain length, and the green blood of the grass on his hands. That was too real. Small, clockwork things like scorpions of brass and silver moved across the floor, their claws the only sound in the room.

Sparrow said, "We're not yours."

But you have come to this place. My place.

"Where are we?" Fielding swallowed, staring into the fire as he spoke. "Are we dead?"

We are in a place of hope, which death does not allow.

"Hope…"

There is much to do. This house is not as it seems.

Fielding thought: *Narnia. Nothing's what it seems. Is it?* They would be recruited. Find out the thing's secrets. Fight for it, maybe. Like in the book: swords and chainmail, and talking animals. No Turkish Delight, but did you need it to bribe someone, when you bribed with hope instead? *It'll offer us something… a deal. Or something to sign. In blood perhaps.*

It said, *No blood will be needed. Only come with me, and I shall show you your new duties.*

"Where will we go?" Sparrow moved towards the desk, hesitated, moved back.

Away from here. There is more than you know.

"Can we go home?"

This will be your home.

Fielding could almost see Sparrow's thoughts in a bubble above her head: School, Xbox, baseball. Her little brother, Francis. Their dog Boomerang.

Yes, but, he thought, looking away from her and gazing dreamily into the fire. That fear on her face. *We should be* more *afraid of going home, shouldn't we? Where everything's falling apart. Where the whole world was supposed to throw its weight behind fixing things, and no one did, and they all busted up, squabbling, the protests didn't work, the marches didn't work, nothing worked. They left it to the future. They left it to…*

"No," said Sparrow. "We already have a home. It belongs to us. And we belong to it."

Distantly, as if it were wrapped in a blanket, Fielding gradually sensed that she had taken his hand, and was squeezing it, hard.

He tried to squeeze back. The fire gave a hard, clear warmth that left his back cold; part of him did not want to turn away from it.

I followed you down here, he thought. *Down here, we could... and you're my best friend. You wouldn't leave me. You wouldn't leave the world, either. Would you?*

He looked up, head clearing. "No," he said to the thing. "No. Like she said. We gotta go. Let us go. Make the house let us go."

Why?

"Because there's still work to do back home. That's why."

"Yeah," Sparrow put in, tugging on his hand. They backed towards the door, still locked. "Even if the grown-ups won't do it."

"Even if there's only a year left."

"Even if."

Silence, and a sense of thunderheads, of anger filling the room like the pressure and ozone of a big storm far away. Fielding wondered how they could fight back: if they would be attacked by this thing. If this was real enough to leave them buried below the dead power plant.

"Let us go," he said again.

No. You will change your minds. We have ways of...

We?

Nope. The window. He glanced quickly at Sparrow, at the stained glass. It looked sturdy and had lines of lead in it, but you could break even thick glass faster than a door. It was behind the thing though. They would have to split up.

Letting go of her hand was wrenching, but necessary.

One. Two. Three.

He swiftly tugged his backpack off and swung it toward the thing, head turned away, startling himself as he toppled onto the empty chair and fell. His chin slammed into the wooden floor, teeth clacking together, and he rolled over just in time to get his hands over his face as a boiling darkness seethed toward him from the corner of the room, screeching, a swarm, a plague.

And then it stopped short, coalescing into a shivering cloud at the edge of his vision: for while it had been distracted, Sparrow had used his backpack, full of books and water bottles, to smash the window, swinging it like she was aiming for the bleachers.

No! it howled.

Fielding scrambled up over the crumbles of glass and ducked under the thing, leaving the screaming cloud frozen and shrieking, as if the damage to the house were a wound it too had sustained. They hauled each other up and over the wooden sill and onto the slate roof, then down, sliding from angle to angle till they were back on the grass, running through an impenetrable darkness and into a bright moment of pain—a sharp disconnect, a jerk, as if sliding on ice, and then they saw the familiar golden colour of the sky and the open maw of the broken cement wall.

"Wait," he panted as they limped back for their bikes hidden behind the chipped concrete barriers; he felt as if something were still at his back, following him, like the pressure of a predator's eyes when you went camping—like the unseen eyes of a cougar. "Wait. Sparrow, wait."

"For *what*?"

"I don't know." He glanced around wildly, though they were alone again. Not even any birds. "Was that real? Did that..."

"Who cares? Maybe we got sour gassed or something. Or maybe it was that fucked-up yogurt. But we gotta go no matter what it was. What are you staying around for?"

This. This. That the secret grass onto which they had fallen was real and not-real, that the broken place that had pulled them in was real and not-real, and he didn't know how it worked, maybe some scientist or something would, but it might be real enough to burn. And he wanted it burned. Dead.

Feverishly, coughing against the dust, eyes streaming, he knelt next to his bike and jerked the battery loose. *If it's all that thing's got, if it's all... don't, no, I can't. Think of the smoke.*

One more thing to fix. Come on.

That's how we got here in the first place!

He looked up when Sparrow shook him, stunned, two ends of wire in his hands and his penknife ready to go. A little cheap plastic-housed thing with THORSBY ELEMENTARY SCHOOL on it. Everyone had the same one.

"Don't," said Sparrow, eyes wide. "Don't. They'll never put it out."

"What?"

"The coal will catch. Look."

He didn't look where she pointed this time, able to see it clearly enough in his head. Yes: the crumbly dark earth the quake had exposed here was both soil and stray bits of coal, and the seam would start on fire if he used the battery to bomb the plant. And who knew how long that would burn or where it would go.

Still, he hesitated, and at last she seized his collar and pulled him away. "Let's just go. Let's go. And do what we said."

"What did we say we were gonna do?"

"The work," she said. "Fix your bike. The work."

They rode back to town just as the sun was going down, and paused on the corner of Sparrow's street.

"*Was* that real?"

"I think so." He gestured around them: the lowering, crimson glare; the grasshopper plague; the yards of stone and dead trees. "Like you said though. This is real, too. And we gotta do the work."

"Okay. See you tomorrow then? To start?"

"Yeah."

He watched her pedal off and turned his hands over, looking at the cuts the glass had made on his palms; then he too turned, and headed for home.

About the Contributors

Winnipegger **BOB ARMSTRONG** has worked as a writer across western Canada. His western, *Prodigies* (Five Star Publishing), was published in 2021, almost a decade after his debut, *Dadolescence* (Turnstone Press). This year's publications include memoirs on cycling (in *Write to Move*) and cancer and comedy (in *Reunion: The Dallas Review*), an essay on Canadian literary westerns (in the *Literary Review of Canada*) and a magical realist take on the pandemic (in *FreeFall Magazine*).

SAMANTHA MARY BEIKO is the author of the young adult fantasy novels *The Lake and the Library, Scion of the Fox, Children of the Bloodlands,* and *The Brilliant Dark* with ECW Press. She is the co-editor of the comic anthology *Gothic Tales of Haunted Love*, and the solo editor of its follow-up, *Gothic Tales of Haunted Futures*. Her short fiction has been anthologized in *Gush: Menstrual Manifestos of Our Times,* and *Parallel Prairies*. Beiko is also the artist and writer for the ongoing creator-owned webcomic, *Krampus is My Boyfriend!*

SHELDON BIRNIE is a writer, reporter, and beer league hockey player who lives in Winnipeg, Manitoba with his wife Clara and their two young children.

DAVID DEMCHUK's debut horror novel *The Bone Mother*, was nominated for the Scotiabank Giller Prize, the Amazon Canada First Novel Award, the Toronto Book Award, the Kobzar Book Award, and a Shirley Jackson Award in the Best Novel category. It won the 2018 Sunburst Award in the Adult Fiction category. His troubling new novel, *RED X*, published by Strange Light/ Penguin Random House, arrived in August 2021.

CHADWICK GINTHER is the Prix Aurora Award-nominated author of the *Thunder Road Trilogy* and *Graveyard Mind*. His short fiction has appeared in many magazines and anthologies, including *Parallel Prairies*. He lives and writes in Winnipeg, Canada, spinning sagas set in the wild spaces of Canada's western wilderness where surely monsters must exist.

PATRICK JOHANNESON writes science fiction and fantasy. His work has been published in *The Arcanist*, *On Spec*, and *Tesseracts* and won the Manitoba Short Fiction contest. Other fascinations include website programming, judo (which he teaches), Canadian and indie cinema, and Norse mythology. He lives in Brandon, Manitoba, with his wife.

LYNNE M. MACLEAN (she/her) was born and raised in Winnipeg, Manitoba, where she began her career as a mental health practitioner. She studied and worked in Edmonton, Yellowknife, and Saskatoon before ending up in Ottawa, Ontario, where she is a community/mental health research consultant. She has had several publications of short fiction and poetry, including in *Augur Magazine, Room Magazine, On Spec Magazine, Podcastle, Speculative North*, and *Stupefying Stories*, among others. She can be found on Twitter @lynnemaclean2 and on her website at www.lynnemmaclean.com.

PREMEE MOHAMED is an Indo-Caribbean scientist and speculative fiction author based in Edmonton, Alberta. She is the author of novels *Beneath the Rising* (Crawford, Aurora, and Locus Award finalist) and *A Broken Darkness*, and novellas *These Lifeless Things*, *And What Can We Offer You Tonight*, and *The Annual Migration of Clouds*. Her short fiction has appeared in a variety of venues and she can be found on Twitter at @premeesaurus and on her website at www.premeemohamed.com.

SHERYL NORMANDEAU hails from Calgary, Alberta, smack dab between the mountains and the prairies. Her work has appeared in several anthologies and magazines, including *Ficta Fabula*, *The Luna Station Quarterly*, *Universe Horribilis*, and *Weirder Science*. She was a shortlisted author for the 2015 Howard O'Hagan Award for Short Stories (Alberta Literary Awards).

Like a magpie, **RHONDA PARRISH** is constantly distracted by shiny things. She's the editor of many anthologies and author of plenty of books, stories and poems. She lives with her husband and two cats in Edmonton, Alberta, and she can often be found there playing Dungeons and Dragons, bingeing crime dramas, making blankets or cheering on the Oilers.

Her website, updated regularly, is at www.rhondaparrish.com and her Patreon, updated even more regularly, is at www.patreon.com/RhondaParrish.

WAYNE SANTOS has been an ad copywriter, a TV scriptwriter, a magazine contributor, an editor, and a freelance writer for too many things on the Internet to count. He is the author of science fiction/fantasy novels, such as *The Chimera Code* and *The Difficult Loves of Maria Makiling*. He is a multi-disciplinary geek with a double major in science-fiction and fantasy, specializations in novels, comics, anime, TV and film, and a minor in video games.

Under no circumstances should he be approached to discuss '80s pop culture unless you are fully aware of the toll this will expend on your remaining lifespan.

LINDA TRINH is a writer of Vietnamese descent, and she writes fiction and creative non-fiction. She explores the intersection of identity with cultural background and spirituality. Her work has appeared in *Prairie Fire, Room Magazine, This Magazine*, and *The Nasiona*. She has been a finalist in the *Malahat Review*'s Constance Rooke CNF contest, and has been nominated for two National Magazine Awards. Linda lives in Winnipeg/Treaty 1 Territory. Twitter: @LindaYTrinh.

About the Editors

DARREN RIDGLEY is a journalist and genre fiction writer. He co-edited, along with Adam Petrash, *Parallel Prairies: Stories of Manitoba Speculative Fiction* (Enfield & Wizenty).

His work has previously appeared in anthologies such as*:* *A Quiet Afternoon 2* (Grace&Victory); *Endless Apocalypse* (Flame Tree Publishing); *Fitting In: Historical Accounts of Paranormal Subcultures* (Mad Scientist Journal); and *Memories of the Past* (Fantasia Divinity). His fiction has also appeared in periodicals such as *Mad Scientist Journal, Empyreome, Polar Borealis*, and *Fantasia Divinity*.

He resides in Winnipeg, Manitoba with his wife Lindsay and their two children.

ADAM PETRASH is a writer from Winnipeg.

He is the co-editor, alongside Darren Ridgley, of the speculative fiction anthology *Parallel Prairies: Stories of Manitoba Speculative Fiction* (Enfield & Wizenty) and the author of the indie novella, *The Ones to Make it Through* (Phantom Paper Press).

His work has appeared in the anthology *Fitting In: Historical Accounts of Paranormal Subcultures*, and in places such *as After the Pause, CHEAP POP, Devolution Z, Fantasmagoriana 2, Lemon Hound, Spacecraft Press, WhiskeyPaper*, the *Winnipeg Free Press*, and other publications.

Editors' Acknowledgements

The editors would like to thank:

Our publisher, Mel Marginet at Great Plains Publications for the opportunity to work together again; our editorial director, Catharina de Bakker, for her masterful attention to detail and for putting the final polish on this collection; our marketing director, Sam K. MacKinnon, for their championing of this book and unwavering support.

Relish New Brand Experience for yet another stunning cover.

All the contributors, without whose stories this book would not be possible. We encourage readers of this book to seek out their books and other stories if you haven't yet done so.

Last but not least, we would like to thank Lindsay and Sarah for their love and support.